When
Ravens
Screamed
Over Blood

For Ruyi

When
Ravens
Screamed
Over Blood

William Vaughan

y Lolfa

Cover design: Sion Ilar
Cover image: iStockphoto/NKTN

ISBN: 978 1 78461 605 2

Published and printed in Wales
on paper from well-maintained forests by
Y Lolfa Cyf., Talybont, Ceredigion SY24 5HE
e-mail ylolfa@ylolfa.com
website www.ylolfa.com
tel 01970 832 304
fax 832 782

Author's Note

Rhydian appears to be the perfect Prince of Dyfed. Much loved by his subjects, he is kind, just, handsome, and seems set for a long and glorious reign. Why then is he driven into exile and treated little better than a leper?

By accident, the Prince incurs the wrath of Anguish, High King of Achren, who demands that he takes his place in a duel against a gigantic opponent. A series of adventures ensues, including the rescue of his sister, the Princess Rhiannon, and an encounter with the ghost of a murdered courtier. Accompanied by his Irish friend, Daire, he enters the Celtic Otherworld, a strange version of life on earth. They experience the joys of love, unaware that a powerful, imperial army is about to invade Britain.

The Prince was inspired by a character and certain magical events in the ancient Welsh tales of the *Mabinogion*. The story also draws upon Irish mythology. The title is taken from a poem in *The Black Book of Carmarthen*, one of the icons of Welsh literature.

1

The Prince

The Prince of Dyfed rode an ash-grey stallion through Welsh countryside so rugged and remote that it was hardly known. Had a colossal hand put the encircling hills in place to hide his people from prying eyes? It was possible, he thought. Months could pass without a stranger stumbling across them.

For a man of twenty years, Rhydian was unusually wise. When he spoke to his subjects, even the lowliest understood. He dispensed justice, and settled disputes, with a kindness which was infectious. His smile shone like the sun, and his slender yet muscular frame, raven-black hair, and green as emerald eyes, were much admired.

The day was sparkling, and he had ridden ahead of his hunting-party so that he could be alone to appreciate it. He entered a forest which was a feast of early-autumn colour. Dappled sunlight drifted through gold, tawny and red leaves. The world looked magnificent, and he felt at ease with his lot in it.

A stag suddenly leapt from the undergrowth destroying his daydreams. The Prince could hear his hounds yelping and barking in the distance, so he whistled and called for them, but a pack of devilish-looking dogs appeared instead. Their white coats glittered like snow, their eyes and ears glowed red as burning coals, and their paws flew so fast that they left scorch-marks on the soil.

Rhydian gazed in disbelief. He had never seen such animals, and wondered why there were no huntsmen with them to put the deer out of its misery. Within seconds, the terrified creature was being torn apart. Instinctively, he kicked his horse's flanks and charged at the hounds, driving them away with his spear. Then he dismounted, drew his sword and plunged it into the twitching animal's throat to end its death throes.

As warm blood spurted onto his hand, a middle-aged man, cloaked in crimson, rode up and berated him. 'You impudent knave! To drive away my dogs after they took that beast, and then to call it your own! For your insolence, I will do you more harm than the value of a hundred stags!'

The stranger's face was livid and his tone so threatening that Rhydian stopped to apologise. 'Sir, I beg your pardon, though mischief was the last thing on my mind. You are obviously a person of standing. Pray tell me your name and rank, and I will offer some means by which I can atone for my error. I am Rhydian, Prince of Dyfed.'

'And you are addressing Anguish, the High King of Achren,' declared the stranger in a resounding, self-important fashion. 'You can only gain forgiveness by coming to my country and defeating a cur named Leare in mortal combat. He is a formidable warrior, intent on usurping my throne.

'A magical power allows me to exchange our appearances. I propose to take your form and will rule Dyfed. You can assume my features and fight the traitor for me. Next midsummer's day, we shall return here, and resume our rightful positions. What do you say?'

Although Rhydian intended to keep his word, he protested, 'But, Sire, I have no idea where Achren is!'

Anguish snorted, and dismissed the objection with an imperious wave of his hand. 'I will show you a secret path to my capital. By the time you reach Annwn, you will look so like me that even my wife – the most exquisite and intelligent woman in the kingdom – will not realise you are an imposter. Are we agreed? Will you do battle with the evil one?'

'I so swear,' the Prince promised.

The High King, whose wild windswept hair resembled antlers, seemed strong and powerful. Leare must be built like a giant to make such a man quake with fear.

*

For more than two days, much of it in silence, Rhydian rode in the wake of the monarch's piebald steed. There was no sign of the strange dogs, so he ventured to ask about them.

'My hounds possess powers of running beyond your imagining. They will already be safely kennelled in Annwn,' Anguish explained.

Over sheep-scattered hills, down stream-filled valleys, through grassland, bracken and woods, the royal pair travelled. When they came to a barn, on the edge of a forest, they dismounted. Its interior was dim and still, and heavy with the scent of hay. They tethered and fed their horses. Then the High King took the crude lantern which lit the gloom, held it before him and they began to trek along a narrow trail through the trees.

On a night when the moon rarely showed her face, spits of rain straddled the shrieking wind and withered leaves whirled around their heads. The Prince, like a dutiful page, continued to follow in the monarch's footsteps. Though cold, wet and hungry, he sensed that their journey was near its end.

They emerged from the woodland to see a row of lights wavering in the distance. Anguish pointed at them and boasted, 'Those are the torches on the ramparts of my fortress, the finest you will ever lay eyes upon. Mark well the path we take for, tomorrow, you must follow it alone. Now, let us return to the barn for some rest.'

When the Prince woke from a deep sleep on a bed of straw, his guide had already drifted into the night. Before entering his new kingdom, Rhydian strode through the glistening grass, around each stalk of which a strand of shimmering cobweb seemed to have been woven, to a stream to wash. He bent forward to splash water onto his face and broke into a sweat. The High King's reflection was staring up at him.

2

Queen Elen

Achren's capital was situated on a low hill surrounded by ditches and high palisades. Within its walls were dozens of thatched huts where the townsfolk lived in safety. The palace was made of wood, wattle and daub, but it dwarfed the other buildings. The towers at each of its corners, consisting of four floors crowned with copper-covered spires, were unrivalled in Wales.

The great hall was twice the length and height of the Prince's own, and from its ceiling shone stars and a silver moon. The walls were adorned with round shields embossed in gold, crossed spears and axes of bronze. All glinted in the flickering light of the fire and tallow candles. The high table, where the royal family sat, was ornately carved from oak, and both thrones were gilded and studded with rubies. Rhydian was open-mouthed at such splendour.

The local men were clothed in loose-fitting, long-sleeved shirts, tight hose tied above the ankles, and cloaks dyed brilliant colours which were fastened at the shoulder. Most of them wore flat, felt hats, but their wives' hair was uncovered and tied in a knot at the back of the neck.

The women's gowns were crossed in lines like tartan, and decorated with amber beads and gold brooches. Their mantles were longer than the men's so they could be swept over their heads in the wind and rain.

With few exceptions, the people were handsome but when Elen, the Queen of Achren, entered the hall, her face and figure drew an audible gasp of admiration from the Prince. She was tall, slim and shapely. Long fair hair, tied into two plaits, draped down her shoulders and breasts, and ended in balls of gold. Hyacinth-blue eyes contrasted vividly with a pale, smooth skin. When she spoke, Rhydian noticed her pink as pomegranate lips and even, white teeth. At first sight, he was smitten with a yearning he had never experienced before.

'Welcome, my lord,' the Queen said, but her embrace was tepid, and her kiss barely brushed his cheek. 'The palace has been very quiet in your absence. To honour your return, I will order the preparation of a banquet which will bring an end to our peace.' As with the courtiers, she seemed content to accept that the man before her was the High King for he was as like Anguish as an identical twin.

Rhydian disliked deceit, and was almost grateful for the lack of warmth in her greeting, though there was also a pang of regret that their lips had not touched. 'I thank you for this courtesy, my lady. In fact, the long journey has left me weary, and I do not feel as well as you look,' he said, but his clumsy attempt at a compliment was ignored.

A splendid feast was held later. Salmon, followed by venison, boar and roasted vegetables were served on platters of bread. Fountains of wine and ale flowed, until the cry went up, 'A toast to the High King's health! And damnation to all his enemies!'

The Queen remained in her seat. Throughout the course of a meal which ended with cheeses, pears and apples, she spoke only a few words to him. Her indifference was icy and palpable.

The revels continued past midnight when the couple headed for their bedchamber. Though tempted by her beauty, the Prince was determined not to take advantage of another man's wife, so he was relieved to see a bolster down the middle of the bed. This, it was clear to him, was to be regarded as a wall. The High King was to lie on one side of it, and the Queen on the other. Little love existed in this marriage. Kisses and caresses were things of the past. Elen fell asleep before he could wish her 'a good night'.

The morning air turned Rhydian's skin to goose-flesh when he opened the shutters to stare from the window. In the distance stood a circle of jagged rocks which he somehow knew were of the magical blue stone from the Preseli mountains of Dyfed. Though they made him wistful, he was determined to fulfil his promise and rule this kingdom wisely. If he avoided the Queen by helping the people and hunting the stag, he hoped his months in exile might melt as swiftly as April snow.

*

The Prince's considerate manner soon set tongues wagging. His courtiers were used to a short-tempered tyrant. When a boy, whose face was more freckled than a thrush's breast, slipped and spilt a bowl of *cawl* intended for the High King, they anticipated a tirade of rebukes. The whimpering servant expected a box on the ear.

Instead, Rhydian picked him up, ruffled the curls on his head and said, 'Calm yourself. A tumble does not warrant such a torrent of tears. Let me wipe them away.'

At this unaccustomed kindness, the lad threw his arms around his master, hugged him and said, 'Bless you, my lord.'

His blessing drew a smile from the Prince which lit the great hall like a slanting shaft of sunshine on a winter's day. 'And may the gods protect you,' he replied.

By the time the happy youngster ran off, the Queen's eyes were a little watery. She had watched her husband's every movement, gesture and expression, and put a finger to her lips to warn the courtiers against interfering. Her hands were clasped together, as if in prayer. For once, she felt proud of him.

Elen had been ordered to marry Anguish by her father. She had been given no say in the matter, and had only laid eyes on her betrothed at the wedding ceremony when she was disappointed to encounter a man older and plainer than herself. Time, she hoped, would allow her to fall in love with him, but the High King's selfishness, which she considered the most ignoble of traits, ensured her feelings had turned into contempt.

Without warning or explanation, his recent decision to shave off his scruffy beard, and to trim and brush his hair, had made him look younger, almost handsome. Fitfully, their eyes began to make contact, and Elen saw an attractive hint of green in his irises which she had not noticed before.

Far more important was the change in his ways. A new, gentler atmosphere began to pervade the court. Acts of royal generosity became so commonplace that the Queen started to look upon Anguish in a more favourable light. But what had brought about this metamorphosis?

As was her habit, she asked him directly, 'My lord, while you were away from the last hunting-party, did anything untoward happen? You were lost for several days and, since then, you have displayed a more considerate manner of ruling your people of which I much approve.'

The embarrassed Prince was unsure how to answer her as he found it almost impossible to lie. Wearing a blush on his cheeks and a few beads of sweat on his forehead, he muttered, 'Nothing out of the ordinary, my lady. I needed time alone for reflection – which may, I suppose, have had some beneficial effects – so paid little heed to the passage of the hours. That is all.'

To change the subject, he asked more candidly, 'Can

you remind me when I am expected to meet Leare in combat? What sort of man is he?'

The Queen's eyes narrowed. She was astonished by this unlikely explanation, and puzzled by his queries. The High King was far more knowledgeable about martial matters than she was. Perhaps, she mused, he has received a blow to the head. Something had affected his nature for the better, and his memory for the worse!

'You might be easier in your mind if you had not asked such questions,' she warned. 'The brute has promised to execute his challenge on *Calan Gaeaf*, the first day of winter. Long ago, Britain was ruled by a race of giants much bigger and uglier than humans. Leare must be their descendant for he bears both characteristics. He is reputed to be a fearless warrior, so it might be wise to spend more time practising your military skills. You have neglected them, of late.'

The heat at Rhydian's temples faded, and the blood drained from his face. His mouth became too dry to speak so he nodded in agreement, and sighed. He had hoped to live longer.

The Queen gave a soft intake of breath when she saw his features contort into a misshapen mask. Anguish had never looked so sad and forlorn. She wrapped her cloak tighter to keep out a sudden chill in the air. Almost without realising it, Elen found herself feeling concern for her husband's fate.

3

Anguish

'Long live the Prince! Long live the Prince!'

A hubbub of cheering and clapping greeted Anguish when he entered Arbeth, Dyfed's capital, laden with venison and boar. As he rode past, the people were puzzled that he did not glance at them, wave or smile, but their ruler looked as youthful and handsome as ever.

The High King was astonished by the fervour of their welcome. At home, his reception was a sullen silence at best, hissing and booing at worst. To be greeted with shouts of acclamation was a novel experience. He had never bothered to display a friendly feeling, or say a kind word, to his own subjects, and so had received none in return. The warmth here was impossible to ignore. Even his hard heart was softened by it.

The peasants were poor. That much was obvious. They were smaller in stature and darker than those of Achren. Their clothes were made from a coarse material which was patched and threadbare. The huts were tiny and smoky, though they often seemed to resound to the sounds of song and laughter.

Anguish was aghast when he saw the palace. No towers. No spires. A plain and poky great hall. Gold and rubies notable only by their absence. Everything was of an inferior quality beneath the dignity of a High King.

In beauty and dress, his new courtiers were no match for the old ones. They also had the annoying habit of talking and laughing so freely in his presence that he would be obliged to bellow, 'Hold your tongues! Is everyone in Dyfed deaf? Speak only after I have given you permission to do so. I am tired of telling you this.'

A deathly hush would follow as his orders were always obeyed with a good grace. No matter how unreasonable he was, his people reacted with loyalty and patience. The High King found their cheerfulness irksome. Sometimes, his face would blanch, he would shrug his shoulders, and stalk off to keep his own company.

The courtiers were convinced that the Prince must be in pain. What other reason could there be for his odd behaviour? Until he recovered from this malady, they agreed among themselves to be more considerate than normal in their dealings with him. And everyone prayed to the Celtic gods for the restoration of his thoughtful and generous nature.

*

Rhydian had a sister, the Princess Rhiannon, who also owned dark lustrous tresses, a dazzling smile and sparkling eyes. Only concern about the deterioration in the Prince's character, and a sudden loss of interest in his appearance, clouded her beauty. Dark stubble had begun to sprout from his chin, a comb no longer touched his hair, and a sour smell had started to follow him around the palace.

She asked, 'Brother, did an accident or sickness befall you while you were absent from the recent hunt? You were lost for a long time, and your good humour seems to have deserted you.'

'Let me be the judge of that!' Anguish snapped. 'My disposition is its normal self.'

'Oh, Rhydian, it is not!' the shocked Princess retorted. 'I have never known you to be quick-tempered, nor so rude and hurtful to your people. You are unwell. Please do me the courtesy of the truth.'

The High King groaned, and raised a hand to his furrowed brow. He could not grant her wish, but was weary of the accusation of being ill. Perhaps his life might be easier if he made more of an effort to imitate the Prince's behaviour. How difficult could it be to display a little consideration and care? Uncertain though he was, he decided to put this plan into operation.

After a pause for thought, he lied, 'While I was in the country, sister, I may have caught an ague. My head has been throbbing, and a fever has almost made sleep impossible. This may account for my poor humour. Henceforth, I shall be kinder to my subjects and, as you put it, try to be more like myself.'

The Princess was relieved to hear her brother's

explanation and summoned the royal physician to tend to him. Myrddin, who wore the white robes of a druid and a golden circlet of sacred oak leaves in his cascade of silvery hair, was the fount of all human and spiritual knowledge at court. He sat in the sage's seat at high table which was reserved for the wisest man. Only the most foolhardy ever challenged his judgement or decisions. Matchless in telling the stories of Wales, he was also highly skilled in the preparation and prescribing of herbal potions, several of which he brought to the Prince.

Anguish demanded, 'Are you sure you understand which plants to stir into these concoctions, and which to leave alone?'

'I have been well-trained in the ancient ways, and know my herbs,' Myrddin replied. He added testily, 'Unlike humans, they have fixed properties and rules. These brews are safe to imbibe, my lord. They will ease any pain, aid sleep, and restore your good health.'

And, after drinking them for a fortnight, the High King was almost as good as his word!

On his liverish days, the Anguish of old found it impossible to play the part of a perfect Prince. Then he would still bark at his servants and snap at his courtiers or, even worse, hand down to some wretched peasant a punishment which his crime did not warrant. Nevertheless, such incidents became rarer and rarer.

Just when Princess Rhiannon thought she would never see her brother's sweet face again, Anguish shaved off his unkempt beard and dragged a comb through his unruly hair. She was delighted by the improvement in his looks.

*

On midwinter's day, when Dyfed was in the icy grip of frost and snow, a serving-girl tripped over a dog and broke a bowl of mulled wine intended for high table. As she watched the aromatic liquid seep into the floor, a look of horror crossed her face. She began to shake, and tears tumbled down her flushed cheeks.

The courtiers were no longer sure how their ruler would react to her fall. Displays of petulant anger had become less frequent, but were still known. A strained silence descended upon the court so that the moans of the cruel north wind could be heard.

Eyes turned towards the High King who was looking grave. He stood up and advanced upon the girl, and an apprehensive murmur filled the chamber. Then he put a consoling arm around her shoulders, smiled his once-familiar smile, and kissed the top of her head.

'Let me dry your pretty face,' he said, wiping it gently with a clean napkin. An eruption of cheering shook the great hall's rafters, and rows of icicles plunged from the eaves into the freshly-fallen snow. The return of their Prince's good health and temper were all his subjects had craved for months.

4

The Duel

The first day of November dawned, damp and dreary, and the Prince pondered on the probability of it being his last. Sleep had refused to release him from his wretchedness. He had never felt less like facing the future.

When a youth, he had been taught the skills of warfare and was a talented swordsman, but he lacked physical aggression. His tutor had complained that he did not possess 'a killing instinct'. Why King Anguish had chosen him to be his champion in mortal combat was a conundrum. A number of Achren's courtiers were taller and stronger than he was.

The duel was scheduled for midday, inside the circle of jagged blue stones, a mile or so from the fortress. Before Rhydian departed, the Queen sought him out, and displayed an unexpected concern for his welfare.

She attempted to reassure him, saying, 'My lord, I saw victory in my dreams last night. I witnessed you standing over an enemy whose body was covered in wounds and blood. This means you will triumph today. It is certain that Leare walks in a dead man's shoes!'

The Prince tried to smile at her premonition, but

failed. 'Your words are well-meant, my lady, but I have learnt that dreams do not always come true.'

When he turned to leave, the Queen grabbed his arm, spun him round and, for the first time, kissed him full on the lips. Elen had begun to think it possible that she could tether her heart to his.

Rhydian's face reddened. Shocked and unsure how to respond, he said, 'Your kindness has eased my mind. I truly hope we will meet again.'

*

The Prince rode slowly through the morning mist and entered the stone circus armed with a sword, spear and shield as had been agreed in advance. The High King's helmet, garlanded in gold, sat so uncomfortably on his head that he wanted to discard it, but the two courtiers who were acting as his seconds insisted that it be worn.

A raven suddenly swooped past his face, startling him. In a beating of black feathers, it perched on the tallest of the blades of stone and stared at him with its beady eyes. Morrigan, the Celtic goddess of war, was reputed to take the shape of such a bird when she wanted to witness a battle. The Prince was also aware that ravens screamed with delight when feasting upon the corpses of warriors who fell in combat, an unnerving thought which made his body shake.

Roars, like those of an angry bull, pulsed through the

still air, announcing his opponent's arrival. A towering warrior strode into the ring of death, and Rhydian's knees knocked. The blood gushed from his face when he saw that Leare was almost twice his height. Without any seeming effort, he carried a five-pronged spear in one hand, and a huge shield as black as ebony in the other. A gold-handled sword, longer than a battle-axe, dangled from his waist. His head, much of which was buried in a straw-like beard, had a heavy brow and a cavernous mouth, and was crowned with a three-horned helmet.

Legs wide apart and spitting defiance, Leare dropped his spear, removed the sword from its scabbard and started swinging it round his head. 'You call yourself a High King but you are a villain! The people hate you and cannot wait to see your head on the end of a spike!' he cried, in a frightening frenzy. 'Soon your bones will crunch under my feet and, when they hear of it, every peasant in the land will laugh out loud! Prepare yourself for an eternity of torture and torment in Hades!'

Though Rhydian looked puny, like a boy facing a man, he knew he was lighter and probably faster than his opponent who had plenty of brawn and bravado, but might be less blessed with brains. He decided to try to take his opponent off-guard by launching the first assault.

Like prowling wolves, they began to circle each other. Suddenly, Rhydian darted forward beneath the whirling sword and thrust his own at the giant's leg. It clattered harmlessly against the oval shield which Leare then used to hurl him through the air like a bear throwing off a dog. The Prince crashed onto his back, his helmet skidding across the turf and, for a few moments, his legs waved wildly like those of an overturned woodlouse.

Leare took the chance to charge, aiming a flurry of mighty blows at his foe's unprotected head. Rhydian managed to pick himself up just in time to parry them with his shield. The ogre's sword rang out again and again, his sheer bulk and power forcing the smaller man to his knees. A second swipe from the shield sent the Prince sprawling so that he could only see the solemn sky.

A sword appeared above him grasped in fingers the size of snakes and, for a terrifying moment, he stared into the Temple of Death. Unless he begged for mercy, he knew he must pass through its gates. In duels between the nobility, it was usual to grant such requests, but his enemy raged, 'Mercy? You swore to fight to the death! It is my time to be High King of Achren. And yours to die!'

As the giant prepared to deliver the fatal blow, the sun broke through a cleft in the clouds and blazed into his eyes with a brilliance that blinded him. Only able to see smudgy silhouettes, for a vital second, he hesitated. It was enough. Rhydian rolled aside, and watched the sword plunge into the damp earth. Like a pair of invisible hands, the soil seemed to cling to the blade and Leare was forced to tear desperately at it.

While he did so, the Prince picked up his spear, took careful aim, and hurled it straight through the monster's thigh. A geyser of dusky blood gushed into the air, and Leare toppled over. When he tried to struggle to his feet, the injured leg buckled under his enormous weight.

It was the underdog's turn to stand over his vanquished victim. No plea for clemency came this time. 'Do not leave me here like a stag in a trap!' Leare snarled, baring his brown, broken teeth. 'Put your sword through my heart and end my humiliation!'

'I wish you no harm,' Rhydian insisted. 'Promise never to set foot in my kingdom again, and I will order the royal physician to staunch and salve your wound. Then you must go to your homeland, and treat others as I have done you.'

Droplets of frustration and ignominy, like huge pearls, poured down the giant's cheeks and soaked into his beard. 'I would sooner die!' he cried.

As the life-blood dripped from his leg, Leare grimaced in pain, and his moans gradually became ragged pants for breath. He grew paler, weaker and quieter. Only when he was on the verge of descending into the depths of the Underworld did he accept defeat. In a heartbroken whisper, he agreed to abide by the victor's terms.

With a shriek of disgust that death had not brightened her day, the raven – or goddess – flapped her great wings, circled over the contestants, and soared into a dappled sky of mauve and grey.

5

Time for Truth

'My gallant lord, it does my heart good to see you again! I told you all would end well,' the Queen declared. She was dressed in her finest gown and, when she curtsied, the jewels at her neck flashed brilliantly. She rose, threw her long arms around her husband, and hugged and kissed him, her lips tasting sweet as honey.

Embarrassed by the passion of her greeting, Rhydian's face flushed the colour of a damask rose. He prised himself from her embrace and said, in excuse, 'My back and ribs are sore from the duel, my lady. I am relieved your vision proved a harbinger of good fortune. After Leare's wounds have healed, he will be transported home where he has sworn to live in peace. This meets with your approval, I trust.'

'Such generosity does you credit, my lord. I would have stuck the knave's head onto a stake as a banquet for the ravens! Your aching body needs to be soothed with essence of witch-hazel and healing-oils. I will administer them myself. It is the least I can do.'

When the Prince stripped to the waist, the Queen gaped at his torso. She was delighted to see how much trimmer and tighter it had become since, of late,

Anguish's appetite had also shrunk a lot. Little blood was visible, but ugly bruises were already forming on his left arm and shoulder. He lay down submissively, and allowed her to handle him as she wished. A basket of herbs and lotions was provided by the royal physician, several of which she massaged and stroked into his skin. There was a broad smile on her face, and a tingle in her fingertips, while she did so.

*

That night, the Prince escorted Queen Elen to their bedchamber, as was his custom. To his consternation, the bolster which divided their bed had been removed. He felt intrusive and very awkward. Obviously, the Queen wished to resume intimacy in their relationship.

Rhydian realised he could maintain the pretence he was the High King no longer. He stared into Elen's hypnotic eyes and said, 'It is time I told you the truth, my lady. In spite of outward appearances, I am not your husband.'

It felt good to unburden himself. All the untruths had weighed heavily on his conscience. But he had no idea of the emotional impact of his words.

The Queen's head whirled, and she felt so faint that she had to grab his arm for support. When the giddiness abated, a perplexed frown disturbed the stillness of her face. It sounded implausible but she had already sensed there was something different about her husband. 'Then who are you? And how do you resemble Anguish so closely?' she asked.

'I am Rhydian, Prince of Dyfed, and I journeyed here to fight Leare in place of the High King. By mistake, I did him a wrong, and he demanded that I recompense him for it. He claimed to have the power to exchange our appearances which proved to be true. And, as he wished, I came to rule Achren and combat his enemy, whilst he travelled to Dyfed to reign over my subjects. As we speak, he is doing so, and the people will see a ruler who looks exactly as I once did.'

This explanation fascinated her, and she wanted to know how the stranger, who was standing within touching distance, really looked. 'Have you a likeness of yourself?'

From a leather pouch hidden in his tunic, Rhydian took a piece of parchment and gave it to her. 'This is a worn sketch of me that my sister Rhiannon drew. She is an accomplished artist, but has been a little flattering to her subject.'

The portrait had been coloured in watery paint and revealed the green of the Prince's eyes. When Elen saw them, and recalled the hint of emerald she had recently noticed in her husband's eyes, she accepted that this was, indeed, a picture of the young ruler of a Welsh principality.

She held it in her slender fingers for a time, and

seemed reluctant to let it go. Before handing it back, she asked, 'Now that you have vanquished the villain, Leare, will you return to your own country?'

'Having sheathed my sword, I would like to hasten home, my lady,' he confessed, 'but I have pledged to remain in Achren until midsummer's day. I shall send a message to the High King informing him that his enemy is defeated, and suggest our agreement be brought to an early end.' Looking at the bed, he added, 'It seems you would like to lie with your real husband again.'

A frown crossed the Queen's face because this was not what she wanted. She shook her head and said, 'Of course, you must inform Anguish of today's victory, my lord, but there is no need to break your word on my account. The truth is that I do not love my husband as a wife ought. I see from this drawing that you are a well-favoured man, but you are yet more becoming by nature. Even if you are unwilling to take me in your arms, I should prefer to spend more time with you than him.'

The Prince was unsure how to respond to this admission, and swiftly tried to unravel his thoughts. He had a deep fondness for her, and the idea of completing his task now seemed rather a pleasant prospect. He replied, 'If that is your heart's desire, my lady, I shall remain with you till next summer. Perhaps the bolster should be restored to its rightful place. Temptation is the fiercest foe of all.'

Then he smiled and added, 'In the privacy of our

bedchamber, will you grant me the privilege of calling you Elen?'

The Queen looked happy, and touched his hand. 'That would please me… Rhydian.'

6

Rhiannon's Suitor

Tales of the Princess Rhiannon's beauty had spread abroad, and from every corner of Wales, and as far afield as Cornwall, Brittany and Ireland, suitors started to come in search of her hand. She had felt the warmth of just eighteen summers and was in no hurry to marry. In her mind's eye, too many wives conjured the image of songless birds in cages.

One sunlit afternoon in May, a russet-haired chieftain, by the name of Llwyd ap Gwyn, arrived at court from the island of Ynys Môn in Gwynedd. Though tall and well-built, he was so vain and boastful about his military prowess that Rhiannon considered him a buffoon, and felt uneasy in his company.

'Sir, you seem to have accomplished remarkable feats for one of tender years,' she told him. 'Truth to tell, I am not in search of a warrior for a husband. A man of more peaceful and artistic leanings is my preference, but I thank you for your kind offer, and feel sure that a talented person such as yourself will soon find acceptance elsewhere.'

Rhiannon was wearing a deep green gown which complemented her eyes. Embroidered in gold, it revealed her slender figure and soft, pale shoulders and arms. Her dark good-looks had captivated the nobleman who was smitten with a powerful desire to make her his own.

He was also unaccustomed to being denied and warned, 'Reject me, and you would live to regret it!'

For a few moments, there was an appalled silence in the great hall, but the Princess was also of a determined disposition. Even more firmly, but still politely, she refused his proposal. 'Sir, you are handsome enough, I grant you, but you are not what I am looking for in a husband.'

At these words, the distraught suitor decided that he would return before long and compel this exquisite, if stubborn, woman to become his bride. Dyfed was poorly-armed and defended. It would be straightforward.

*

In the span of weeks rather than months, Llwyd descended from Gwynedd at the head of a thousand foot-soldiers and a hundred horsemen. Under the veil of night, his army surrounded Arbeth and, when darkness yielded to dawn, King Anguish – still in the guise of Prince Rhydian – discovered that his hill fort had been besieged. The strength of the enemy forces also meant he was heavily outnumbered.

He summoned the Princess to the wooden ramparts. Together, they stared over the deep, dry ditch which was keeping them safe for the time being, and watched as tents were erected, fires lit and ever more archers, infantry and cavalry arrived. Swords were sharpened, and feathers glued to arrows. Rhiannon could smell the aroma of roasting meat, and see sparks from the campfires, drifting in a breeze which ruffled her long hair.

Out of the morning mist, the commander himself emerged in a chariot made of wicker and wood, and armed with bronze sickles protruding from its wheels. Clearly in his element, he looked impressive in a long, red cloak. He was brandishing a great, grey spear in one hand and a silver-studded shield in the other. Drawn by two black horses, the charioteer drove him round his troops to roars of approval, and boisterous blasts on hunting-horns.

'A message has arrived from that villain yonder, demanding you become his wife,' explained the High King. 'Otherwise, he will lay siege to our capital, and starve the people to death. We are unprepared, and have laid in no supplies. Hunger will soon make us weak.

'I have heard he is a dragon in battle, and there is the look of victory on his face. Before the next full moon, there will be many wives crying bitterly over the mangled bodies of their husbands. What do you suggest?'

Rhiannon's heart sank like a stone. Though shocked by her brother's defeatist tone, it was hard to disagree with it. The encircling enemy had appeared so suddenly, and silently, that their situation did seem hopeless. She wanted to reply, 'Drive the barbarians into the Irish Sea!' Instead, she braced herself for disappointment and asked, 'How great is his superiority?'

'Ten to one, and they are better armed,' the High King exaggerated.

'The only banner I wish to see flying over Arbeth is yours, Rhydian, but you must not lead your men to certain death on my account,' she insisted. 'I will agree to go with the knave and become his bride, but only if he promises to wait a month until the marriage. You must follow us, and find a means of rescuing me before the ceremony takes place. Pursue this plan, and protect your people.'

As Anguish was no hero, he leapt at her offer. Wide-eyed with gratitude, he cried, 'Sister, you are so selfless, an example to us all! Your scheme will avoid a slaughter.'

*

When a messenger arrived at the invaders' camp to inform Llwyd of Rhiannon's proposal, he crowed, 'Wonderful! I have what I want! And without shedding one drop of blood!' Nothing delighted him more than getting his own way, and the Princess was the prize he desired above all others. He readily assented to her request to delay the nuptials for a few weeks.

To celebrate their victory, he ordered that his men be

given an extra ration of ale. Another instruction went out to dismantle the cairn of stones which had been built prematurely as a memorial to those slain in the siege.

*

Within hours, the Princess found herself heading north towards the mountains of Snowdonia in the belief that Rhydian was riding in her wake. She trusted her brother implicitly. The High King was, in fact, galloping eastwards for his long-planned rendezvous with the Prince.

7

Myrddin's Game-bag

Winter snows had long melted. Spring blossoms had bloomed and blown away in the breeze. Midsummer's day approached. The Prince mounted his stallion and prepared to ride for the spot where he had put the stag out of its misery, and incurred the High King's anger.

In the months since he had defeated Leare, Rhydian had become so popular with the people of Achren that, whenever he passed by, he was greeted with cheers. In looks and character, their ruler had altered so dramatically that it seemed as if they had a new, and much better, one.

The Queen's eyes were puffy and tear-stained when she bade the Prince an emotional farewell. The yearning for him had grown strong, and parting was painful. 'You are the sweetest and loveliest of men,' she sobbed. 'I will miss you more than you will ever know. May the gods keep you safe from harm, and smooth the way before you.'

Rhydian had treated Elen with the same sort of love as Rhiannon, and they had become devoted. Speaking was a struggle. 'Somehow, I know we will meet again, my lady,' he whispered. His green eyes prickled, but he managed to suppress the tears. The time had come to head for his homeland.

*

With just a guide for company, he galloped from Annwn. When they neared the agreed meeting-place on the borders of Dyfed, he instructed the servant to tether his horse, and wait for him, so that he could meet the High King alone.

Though punctual, Anguish was barely recognisable. His unkempt beard had been replaced by a smooth chin, and a comb had tamed his wild hair. Only his piebald stallion looked the same. When the High King greeted him in his unmistakable manner, Rhydian assumed that his own features had returned to normal. 'Prince, it is a pleasure to see you again! For defeating Leare, and ruling Achren, I shall forever be in your debt. My time in Dyfed has taught me much. Thanks to your example, I have become a more thoughtful monarch, and it is my intention to continue to emulate your ways in future. You will find,' he added, a little pompously, 'that I have left your poor principality more prosperous than I found it.'

'Sire, it is a relief to hear all is well with my subjects. I have done my best to make your kingdom more contented than it once was. As you promised, I discovered your wife is the loveliest of women, but you may rest assured that I have always acted properly towards her.

'The Princess Rhiannon is in good health, I trust.'

The High King's smile turned into a scowl. His face darkened and the veins at the side of his forehead protruded. He admitted, 'I fear I have bad tidings on that score. She has been taken – against her will – to Ynys Môn, by a nobleman who has lost all reason because of unrequited love. He intends to make her his bride within the month.'

'And you allowed such a thing to happen?'

King Anguish licked his dry lips, and a strident tone entered his voice. 'We had no choice in the matter! The chieftain, Llwyd ap Gwyn, besieged Arbeth with an army of overwhelming power. When I offered to attack it, your brave sister insisted she would prefer to go with him than risk the slaughter of your subjects. She is counting on you to come to her rescue. You must ride for Gwynedd directly!'

Without a word of farewell, the High King dug his heels into the horse's flanks and cantered away.

Rhydian considered it unwise to head into the mountains of the north until he had sought the advice and assistance of his cleverest counsellor.

*

The scent of drying rose petals, herbs and ointments greeted him when he burst into Myrddin's chamber. Entering it was like a warm embrace. The royal physician seemed unsurprised by his arrival and, before Rhydian could utter a word, said, 'You are weary, my lord. Tomorrow will be soon enough for you to begin your journey to the island of druids which is where you will find the Princess.'

'I am exhausted but, before my eyes close, have you any spells or incantations for me? Without their help, I do not know how I can save Rhiannon.'

The sage stroked his beard, looked studiously down his long nose and replied, 'People overrate the powers of magic, my lord. Few mortals possess them. A Force for Good – created by the gods of light and life – does exist, of which you are a devoted disciple. In you, it is instinctive, like a sixth sense. Goodness oozes from your bones. It will help you overcome a young man who seems to be a follower of the Force for Evil – created by the demons of darkness and death – which also stalks the land.'

Myrddin crossed the room, and rummaged in a wooden chest. At length, he took out a worn game-bag. When he held it up, it fell open and looked large enough to hold the carcasses of a couple of wild boar. He said, 'Take this, and it will enable you to save your sister.'

Rhydian's smooth forehead creased. 'How could such a thing be of any use?' he asked sceptically.

'That is not given to me, my lord. Continue to believe

in the Force for Good, and this piece of leather will ensure your success. Whenever you need help, simply open it and you will know what to say and do.'

8

The Fox

On the eve of his marriage, a banquet was held in Llwyd's great hall which was overflowing with guests and members of his household. The betrothed couple, one wearing a grin and the other a grimace, sat at the high table together. Rhiannon was beginning to lose hope, and looked around in a desperate search for her brother. Surrounded by a sea of jovial faces, she felt marooned on an island of loneliness.

Fortified by too much mead, the chieftain rose to make a speech about his noble birth and deeds in battle which was so boastful that it made her wince. 'As I was born in the court of champions and possess the strength of twenty warriors,' he bragged, 'it is fitting that I should make the Princess Rhiannon, the most attractive and accomplished woman in Wales, my wife.' He leered at her and added, 'As a wedding gift, my lady, I shall grant you any wish – within reason and my powers to bestow – that you desire.'

While he was speaking, Rhiannon noticed a beggar, dressed in ragged garments and worn boots, enter the back of the hall. Despite the flour greying his untidy hair, and the soot darkening his chin, there was no mistaking those sea-green eyes!

Cleverly, she replied, 'I have everything I require, my lord. Unlike that poor man,' and she pointed at Rhydian whose features were unknown in Gwynedd. 'Let him crave this boon for himself. His need of it is much greater than mine.'

Llwyd took one look at the vagabond and laughed. 'Very well. Come hither, peasant, and tell us your wish. Remember, it must be reasonable and within my ability to allow.'

The Prince walked forward, opened the game-bag which he had been carrying over his arm, and said, 'I am half-starved, my lord. All I ask is for this to be filled with meat.'

The nobleman was relieved by such a modest request and ordered that it be granted. Servants brought haunches of venison and sides of wild boar from the kitchens but, when they placed the meat into the leather sack, it remained empty. Everyone in the hall was astonished, and some began to cry out, 'How can this be?'

By the time Llwyd asked the beggar the same question, the smile had disappeared from his face.

For a moment, the Prince hesitated, unsure how to reply. Then he held up the bag and said, 'Until a great lord, possessed of land and riches and capable of fighting twenty men alone, treads the food down with both his feet, this can never be filled.'

The braggard roared, 'That is an exact description of me!'

Rhiannon egged him on. 'So it is, my lord! Do this kindness for the old man.'

'Gladly I will!' the chieftain shouted, and straightaway put his big feet into the sack. No sooner had he done so than Rhydian pulled it over his head and tied the mouth shut. Llwyd began to shout and struggle to get out. His men grabbed the Prince and demanded he release their lord but, when he did as he was told, the bag contained nothing but a fox!

One of the soldiers seized the peasant by the throat and snarled, 'Restore our master to us, or I will slit open your belly and dance upon your innards!'

Rhydian gasped, 'Kill me... and you will never see your lord again... But I will return him safely to you... if you promise to release the Princess Rhiannon... and abandon all false claims to her hand in marriage... I am the Prince of Dyfed... and will die rather than leave this place without my sister!'

This ultimatum infuriated the guard so that his eyes glared from the depths of their sockets. He dragged Rhydian towards the fire, which was set on some flagstones in the centre of the hall between the two long trestle-tables, and roared, 'I am going to roast you like a pig!'

'No, you will not!' a lady's deep voice boomed. 'Unhand the Prince.' The order came from a tall woman whose face was notable for its high cheekbones. Her once-auburn hair was now largely grey. She wore a cloak dyed the deepest blue which was fastened at the shoulder by a magnificent silver brooch. The Lady Olwen possessed such a commanding presence that the hall fell silent. 'My only son is far from perfect, but I love him. I have already lost my dear husband, and cannot bear to enter old age alone. A dead man will not be able to turn that wild animal back into my child.

'Prince, you are welcome to your sister. She has contempt in her heart for Llwyd. I warned him against marrying her, but he is too reckless to heed anyone's advice, especially his mother's. If I set you free, do I have your word that you will ensure his safe return?'

'Madam, you have my solemn promise. I am an honourable man and have no wish to harm your family. Feed and water the creature for twenty-four hours after our departure, and then place it into the bag. As soon as you do so, your son will be restored to normal. By then, we will be far away and you need never see us again.'

'So be it! Let them go! They are not to be molested nor followed,' the Lady Olwen instructed. She clenched her fists and added defiantly, 'Understand this, Prince, no mother ever loved her son more than I do mine. If you break your word, I will send such an army against you that the slaughter in Dyfed will be long remembered.'

With that threat ringing in their ears, the Prince and Princess departed.

*

For a night and a day, Llwyd was imprisoned in absolute darkness like a black shroud. No light, no noise penetrated it. He was too petrified to move or speak. When he emerged into the light, and the paralysing fear was overcome, relief swamped over him. He fell into his mother's welcoming arms, and began to weep like a baby.

9

A Change of Heart

Queen Elen was dreading her real husband's return. She was the only person in Achren to know that the just and generous man who had ruled them for the past nine months had been the Prince of Dyfed. The thought of sharing her life with an irritable bully again, rather than a kindred spirit like Rhydian, filled her with foreboding.

When the High King's distinctive piebald clattered into the palace courtyard, Elen was shocked to see that its rider was much neater and leaner than she remembered. Her husband's unruly, hirsute appearance had vanished. The possibility that Rhydian had returned made her heart leap but, when Anguish called to the servants to deal with his horse, there was no mistaking the different tone of voice.

He marched into the great hall, and a yearning look appeared in his eyes as soon as he saw the Queen. 'It is a pleasure to see you again, my lady,' he declared.

Elen could not bring herself to embrace him. Instead she curtsied and said, 'Welcome, my lord. I hardly recognised you. What has happened to your much-loved beard?'

The High King had forgotten how magnificent his

wife was! He had been stupid to take her beauty for granted. The desire to kiss that lovely face, which made such a perfect setting for those sapphire eyes, and run his fingers through the golden hair draping over her swan-white shoulders, almost overwhelmed him. He wished he had bought her a Welsh gold necklace to wear with that gown of purple braid. A miserly mistake, he regretted. Elen, he now realised, was far more worthy of love than he was.

Her question had taken him aback as both he and the Prince had been clean-shaven at their recent meeting. Confused, he hastily ventured, 'You have complained many times about my shaggy locks so, while I was away, I decided to shear them. Just to please you, my lady.'

His wife gave him a sharp, disbelieving look and decided to test his honesty again. 'And do you remember how you humiliated Leare by tugging at his nose when he lay helpless?'

Anguish had no idea how to answer this because he had not witnessed the duel. Her interrogation made him feel like a worm wriggling on a fisherman's hook. It sounded an unlikely thing for the Prince to do. He was tempted to laugh and try to change the subject, but in the court at Arbeth he had become accustomed to being truthful, and it was a habit he now found difficult to break.

After a pause, he confessed, 'I did not defeat Leare.'

The Queen stared at him and sniggered. 'Your

memory is playing tricks, my lord! I tended your bruises myself.'

The High King rubbed his twitching hands together and admitted, 'They were those of another man.'

'Do not tease me! Explain yourself,' Elen demanded, desperate to know if her husband would tell the truth.

'Rhydian, Prince of Dyfed, vanquished him…'

Before he could continue, his wife interrupted, 'The charade is over! There is no need to go on. Rhydian himself told me of your exchange of titles and roles months ago.'

'Then why did you not say so?'

'Because I expected you to lie, and take the credit. It is in your nature to do so.'

'Your rebuke is well-deserved. The horrors of Hades terrified me. Though I wished the Prince well and sensed he was a fine man, I was indifferent to his fate. If the giant had been victorious, I would have continued ruling Dyfed.'

'And left me mourning you!' she exclaimed.

He laughed hollowly. 'Be honest, my lady, would you have grieved over my death? Or would it have been a blessed relief?'

Elen's face and neck flushed pink at the accuracy of his suspicions.

The High King saw her embarrassment and remarked frankly, 'We both know the truth of the matter, but believe me when I say I am a changed man. The selfish and deceitful wretch you hated, no longer exists.

'The Prince told me you have remained faithful. Your fidelity is laudable because your married life with me has been a miserable one. I concede this and am ashamed of it. My time in Dyfed has taught me to respect everyone, down to the lowest peasant. I have learnt to copy Rhydian's way of treating his people because I now realise that dispensing justice fairly, and being kind, matter more than anything else in a monarch. No doubt, he ruled Achren in such a manner.'

'It has never been governed so well nor been more harmonious,' the Queen insisted. 'And we have gained a good friend.'

'If that is the case, I will do my best to be like him. Even a pale imitation of the Prince is sure to be a great improvement upon the King I used to be. Give me the chance, I beg you my lady, to show how much I have altered!'

Though touched by his impassioned speech, the Queen was well aware that words require little effort. She replied, 'A fair promise, my lord. Very fine. If your actions come close to matching your claims, I shall be delighted. Let us hope your change of heart is more substantial than some mirage in a distant desert.'

*

Apart from the Queen, only his hunting-dogs realised that King Anguish had ever been away. They were overjoyed to meet their master again. Blood-red noses and ears quivered with excitement at his return. Barking loudly, they bounded up to him and rubbed themselves against his outstretched hands. He patted their heads as best he could, saying, 'At least you are pleased to see me! A man could have no finer companions, but I will soon have some with whom I can converse.'

*

The High King did all he could to reconcile himself to his subjects. So deeply had he become imbued with the Force for Good that he kept his promises and more. So insistently did the voice of conscience speak to him that the peasants of Achren came to trust his judgement and accept his decisions. They had ceased calling him 'Anguish the Tyrant' under the Prince's rule. As everything continued as before, they eventually replaced this title with 'Anguish the Just'.

One night, a brilliant full-moon shed its light over the palace of Annwn, touching the copper-clad spires with a reddish-gold glow, and illuminating the royal couple's way to their bedchamber. When Anguish saw that the bolster had been removed, he placed his hands gently on his wife's shoulders and drew her to him. He could feel her heart beating giddily against his chest. A little dazzled by the moonlight, he looked again at the bed to make sure his eyes were not deceiving him. Then they kissed, and a shudder of gratification coursed through Elen's body.

10

Mound of Modron

'Rhydian, it is time you found a wife, and provided Dyfed with a son and heir,' his sister asserted. 'I should welcome the company of some nieces at court too.'

The Prince wondered if it were possible that there could be someone else in Wales as lovely as Elen, but replied, 'Nobody has yet captured my heart.'

So Rhiannon suggested, with a light-hearted laugh, 'Perhaps you should take a trip to the Mound of Modron.'

'What is that? I have never heard of it.'

'Oh, Rhydian, you are so unworldly! Sometimes you make me despair. Everyone in Arbeth knows of the Mound.'

He shook his head. 'Genuinely, I do not.'

'Legend has it that the Mound possesses magical powers. Any man who sits upon it, as the sun rises, is said to encounter one of two things: either he receives invisible slaps and blows to the head or he sees someone wonderful,' she explained. 'Modron is a short ride away. At the least, it would be an interesting experience.'

'No doubt, sister, but the prospect of being cuffed around the ears has little appeal.'

Nevertheless, the Prince rubbed his chin thoughtfully.

*

He was intrigued enough, a few days later, to ride through the darkness to reach the Mound just before daybreak. He tethered his stallion and clambered up the steep sides of the circular, flat-topped structure which had been created by men centuries earlier.

As he settled on the damp turf, something skittered past his nose and startled him. 'Only a bat,' he assured himself aloud.

The first glimmerings of dawn lightened the sky and he felt uneasy, but no blows assailed him. Then, out of the rising mist, a pure-white horse drifted past. Seated on it, and clad in a shining tunic, was a slim figure with long, golden hair. Rhydian found himself hoping that Elen, whose image often glowed in his mind, had come to him.

The horse was ambling, so he slithered down the Mound and began to chase after it but, no matter how fast he ran, he could not close the gap. When his heart began to hammer, and his breath was quite gone, he gave up and watched the horse and its rider disappear.

Fascinated by the mysterious lady, the Prince rode to the Mound the following night. This time, he left his stallion at its foot. When the same events occurred, he scrambled down the slope, mounted his horse and kicked it into a gallop. But, however fast he rode, he still could not catch her up. In despair, he called out, 'Please stop! I mean you no harm, and wish to talk to you.'

At once, the horse came to a halt. Its owner turned to Rhydian and said, 'I will gladly wait for you. It would have been better for your steed if you had asked me to do so earlier as I am only allowed to speak when I am spoken to.'

The Prince listened in gaping astonishment to this explanation because the person who gave it was not a beautiful maiden, as he had supposed, but a slender youth several years younger than himself.

After a few tongue-tied moments, he asked, 'Is there any reason why you cannot speak freely?'

'My father made it a requirement of my banishment,' the young man replied.

Rhydian was perplexed. 'Then who is your father, and why has he done this to you?'

'My name is Daire, and I am the son of Fergus, King of Ulster. Exile in Wales is a lesser punishment than his original one which was execution.'

The Prince's long eyelashes fluttered and his face darkened. 'You must have committed a very wicked act for your own father to order such a thing! I am Rhydian, Prince of Dyfed, and cannot imagine handing down such a judgement without terrible cause. What did you do?'

'I kissed my friend.'

'That cannot be all.'

'It was, my lord, but Indech was a boy.'

'You kissed a boy?'

'Because I liked him very much, and I thought he felt the same way. I was mistaken. Instead of returning my affection as I had expected, he pushed me away. Then he ran to my father, told him what I had done, and called me vile names.'

'Yes, but why were you sentenced you to death?'

It was Daire's turn to look confused. 'I have just told you the reason.'

'No king could condemn someone to be executed because of a kiss!' Rhydian scoffed in disbelief.

'Well, mine did. He told me I was a disgrace to the royal family, and a stain upon its good name. He called me unnatural, and unfit to be a member of the warrior class which is the only one that can rule in Ireland. When he sentenced me to death, he said it would have been better if I had not been born, and that he never wanted to lay eyes upon me again.'

The Prince listened in stunned silence to this account of King Fergus's judgement. 'What you have told me beggars belief. If your father felt that way, why did he commute your sentence to one of exile?'

'Because the Wee Folk came to my help. I will explain…' Daire added, before he could be interrupted again. 'In Ireland, there is a race of very small folk who live alongside humans. Though we exist peacefully together most of the time, some people despise their tiny neighbours, but I helped any of the Wee Folk I met who were in trouble.

'One day, I picked up an old man, who was little bigger than an infant, and carried him over a stream which was too swollen for him to cross. He thanked me, asked my name, but said no more. I was unaware that he was the most respected bard at the court of the King of the Wee Folk, and had written a poem in appreciation of my small act of kindness which had made me famous there.

'As a result, when the Wee Folk heard about my impending execution, they informed my father that, if he proceeded, they would come to Ulster in a great multitude and visit plagues upon it such as stripping off the ears of corn, letting calves suck the cows dry, and defiling all the wells and ponds. Even the King of Ulster was afraid to incur their wrath, so he said I could live, but must be sent across the Irish Sea where I was to remain for the rest of my life. He also ordered that I must only speak when spoken to first. And that is how I came to be in your principality.'

'You are young and cannot spend your entire existence riding endlessly around Wales,' the Prince pronounced. 'You are welcome to live at my court in Arbeth. I doubt if it is as grand as the one you left in Ulster, but food and shelter and companionship await you there. And, while you remain in Dyfed, it is my command that you speak whenever you want, provided it is appropriate to do so.

Please do me the honour of accepting my invitation. I should be unhappy to leave you here alone.'

Daire's face lit up. 'Many months have passed,' he said, 'since anyone was kind to me. I accept your offer, my lord, with the deepest gratitude.'

11

Kiss of Death

The Princess was startled when Rhydian returned from the Mound of Modron with a young man in tow rather than a prospective bride. Like her brother, she was disgusted by the King of Ulster's treatment of his son, though she was not told the whole story of Daire's kiss.

How handsome the Irishman is, she thought. His slender face, with its golden eyebrows and full pink lips, took her fancy at once. His forget-me-not blue eyes shone like candles. His fair hair swept back from a forehead which was unblemished and smooth like the rest of his pale skin. His body was lithe and lean, without an inch of fat.

Although free to speak whenever he wished, the newcomer was inclined to talk only when addressed, so Rhiannon made a point of asking him questions about life in Ireland. When answering in his sometimes broken Welsh, she enjoyed correcting him, though she was careful to add that his knowledge of her Celtic tongue put hers of Irish to shame. He had the air of a gentle soul, and she began to believe that the Mound had sent her, instead of Rhydian, 'someone wonderful'.

Rhiannon did all she could to attract Daire's

attention. She played the harp and sang love songs for him. She repaired and embroidered his torn tunic. She raided Rhydian's wardrobe so that he looked the part of a prince. She showered gifts upon him, including a leather belt with a silver buckle and a twisted torque of Welsh gold for his neck. She sketched his profile, which became etched on her memory, and made him more attractive than he already was.

Although Daire was flattered by the Princess's interest, he preferred riding and hunting with the Prince. Rhydian was always careful to put his duties before personal pleasure, but the two young men spent most of their spare time together. Even the kind-hearted Rhiannon found herself becoming a little envious of her brother.

*

On one of those rare days in Wales when the sun smiles from a cloudless blue and the skylarks are in full-throat, the Prince and Daire went riding, without the usual train of courtiers. Rhydian wished to speak to his friend privately about Rhiannon's feelings. As they rode away from Arbeth, their faces beamed.

When they had travelled some distance, they fell into chatter about court matters and Rhydian took his chance to say, 'Do you realise that my sister has taken to you very strongly? She finds you pleasing to the eye, and she likes your good nature too.'

The Irish prince had already sensed this. He blushed and said, 'Everyone new seems fair and desirable, my lord. In time, I will become just another face at court.'

The Prince laughed. 'You do not know my sister as well as I do! Her feelings are fixed upon you, and I think she longs to be your wife. If you were to ask for her hand in marriage, I am sure she would agree. And I, of course, would readily give my consent to the match.'

His friend squirmed in the saddle and said, 'The Princess is most comely and charming, my lord, but I do not desire her, and never will. My heart lies elsewhere.'

Rhydian was shocked by the certainty in his voice. 'Would that be in Ireland?'

'No, my lord, but that will remain a secret.' Desperate to change the subject, he yelled, 'Let us see if that nag of yours can keep pace with my mare!' He urged his horse into a full gallop which made his hair flow like liquid gold.

'The day when you outrun me will never dawn!' the Prince rejoined, and a furious race began.

The joy of being young and strong was overpowering. The pair charged along a narrow woodland track, beneath a continuous arch of overhanging trees, until they chanced upon a tranquil, blue-sheened lake edged with rushes. A pair of swans, coupled for life, made the scene seem perfect.

Rhydian called out, 'Enough! The day is like a furnace. Our horses need rest, and to be watered.'

As they pulled on their reins, Daire protested, 'Just as I was about to overtake you, my lord! I am also lathered in sweat, and in sore need of a bathe. A swim would refresh us.'

Having dealt with their steeds, they stripped off their clothes, and stretched them out to dry on the grass. The sun was hot on their naked bodies. They ran into the lake's shallows and began to splash each other like a couple of children. They strode into deeper water and began to swim, though it was cold enough to take their breath away. They tumbled like otters and tugged at arms and legs. They twirled and twisted until their bodies touched.

Abruptly, their horseplay ended. The friends fell silent and still. Daire draped his silky arm around the Prince's shoulders, stared through his eyes into the depths of his soul, and said, 'You are beautiful beyond justice.' He hesitated, then kissed Rhydian on the lips. The Prince drew back but, after only a momentary pause, responded passionately.

Hidden in the woods on the banks of the lake, two horrified courtiers watched them. Dafydd ap Gruffydd and Gareth ap Iwan had disobeyed their master's instructions and followed him in secret, but with the best of intentions. They admired the Prince, and wanted to keep him safe from attack by outlaws or enemies.

'They are young and foolish,' Dafydd muttered. 'This

silliness will pass. It would be best to ignore it. Let us leave them in peace, and ride for home.'

But Gareth had taken fire. His angry face was distorted like a gargoyle and he snarled, 'No! This is such wicked and dishonourable behaviour that it cannot be borne! We had the finest Prince in Wales until that Irishman bewitched him. My blade will drink of his blood when I sever his head from his carcass, and break the evil spell!' So saying, he yanked his weapon from its scabbard and, without removing an item of clothing, charged towards the lake and plunged in.

The embracing couple were now standing up to their waists in water, and did not notice their assailant until he was almost upon them. Gareth's sharp-edged sword shone like a stream in the sun. Too late to evade it, the blade slashed into Daire's upper arm and blood began to gush.

Before the courtier could land a second, more telling blow, Rhydian dived on him, grasped both his wrists, and pushed him so hard that he toppled backwards into the lake. The Prince firmed his grip, and waited several seconds, before hauling him up for air. Then he demanded, 'Will you yield?'

Spluttering and gasping, Gareth swore, 'Not until I have removed that fiend's head!'

Whereupon, Rhydian pushed him beneath the water again and held him there. When he allowed Gareth to surface, he repeated, 'Will you yield?'

'Never!'

The Prince reacted angrily to his stubborn refusal to submit and sent him sprawling for a third time. Even longer elapsed before he pulled his opponent up to breathe. 'Will you yield?' he barked again.

Silence was his answer. Gareth's hanging jaw, and bleached face, told him he had gone too far. He shook the limp victim violently in an attempt to revive him. The Prince was aghast. He had drowned one of his most loyal subjects! Like a wounded dog, he began to howl. A wave of nausea welled up in his gullet and a stinking mess poured from his mouth.

A wild shrieking racket rose above his head. A flock of young ravens was preparing to descend upon the slain courtier's corpse.

Rhydian regained control of himself, fished some stones from the bed of the lake, and weighted Gareth's body with them until it disappeared into the darkness. Forever.

Droplets of sweat dripped from his chin as he helped Daire to dry land where he bound the gory gash, which had not yet begun to congeal, with strips of makeshift bandage torn from his own linen shirt. By the time these stopped turning bright red, his friend's face was pallid from the loss of blood and clammy from shock. He was so weak and dazed that, when he tried to stand to put on some clothes, his legs gave way. Only by clinging to the Prince's arm did he remain upright. At length, they managed to dress and clamber onto their horses to begin a walking-pace ride back to Arbeth where Myrddin could tend Daire's injury properly.

A day of sunshine and kisses had ended in death and tears. The princes remained mute for most of the journey. As they neared the outskirts of his capital, Rhydian confided, 'No-one else knows what has happened to Gareth ap Iwan, and that is how it must remain. Whatever befalls us, Daire, you will be unrivalled in my affections until the day I die. That is a solemn promise.'

12

Rumours and Rebellion

Dafydd ap Gruffydd's horse clattered over the timber bridge into Arbeth. He dismounted and hurried home to his wife, Megan, who was more restrained and sensible than he was. She would offer him good advice. After the appalling events he had witnessed, he was still trembling like a leaf in a storm.

When he told her how the peaceful afternoon had erupted in fury and ended in murder, she refused to believe him. A shocked scowl crossed her podgy face and she cried, 'That cannot be! Our Prince is without equal. He is incapable of such a deed!'

'Trust me, my dear, I thought so too. But, as surely as I am standing before you now, I saw him drown my best friend, a man who would not harm a hair on his master's head. Gareth attacked the Irishman because he was throwing himself lustfully upon the Prince. He did nothing to warrant death, much less such a savage one.'

'Are you sure it was murder?'

'As cold and complete as was ever committed,' Dafydd replied. 'But what should I do about it?' he asked, in a high-pitched voice which sounded odd coming from a big man with a bushy, black beard.

'First, husband, you must tell Gareth's wife she is now a widow. Gwyneth is the mother of two boys and a baby girl. Such dreadful tidings will destroy their lives. She is going to need a shoulder to weep on so I will accompany you. Soon, she will demand redress. Even princes must be held to account for their wicked actions.'

'And many of the nobility would hang you just for saying such a thing,' Dafydd warned.

'If telling the truth is treason, so be it!' Megan rejoined. 'Now we must go to break hearts.'

When she heard Dafydd's account of her husband's gruesome death, there was a stunned silence before Gwyneth's face contorted and crumpled. She fell onto her knees, hammered her fists into the earth floor, and began to shriek hysterically. Her neighbours drew back in fright until the screams subsided into sobs. When she recovered herself, only bloody revenge was on her mind. Nothing short of the execution of the two princes would pacify her.

*

Daylight had departed for other climes, and the air had cooled when the horses of the shirtless Prince and his blood-stained companion clopped into the palace courtyard. Unknown to them, rumours of their kiss, and its fatal consequences, were already flying around the capital.

Daire was unable to walk without the Prince's arm

around him for support. This kindness, and their bedraggled appearance, was interpreted by many as open confirmation of Dafydd's accusations and, for once, there was no rush to help the master.

A stern-faced Myrddin set to work to cleanse and salve Daire's wound. He covered the gore with wadding which he then bound tightly with clean bandages. The patient was also given a foul-tasting concoction of herbs to ease the pain. When finished, the druid asked the Prince, who was carefully observing all his actions, 'May I speak freely, my lord?'

'Of course, Myrddin, I have nothing to hide from the son of the King of Ulster,' he replied, making a point of emphasising Daire's royal lineage.

'Vile allegations, such as I have rarely heard in my long life, are circulating at court. I know you are no more capable of murder than I am of flying, but Dafydd ap Gruffydd has accused you of that heinous crime. He swears he witnessed you drown Gareth ap Iwan.'

Upon hearing this, the Prince experienced a feeling of horror unequalled in his worst nightmare. He found it so difficult to tell an untruth that keeping silent about Gareth's mysterious disappearance would have been well-nigh impossible. To invent lies about his death was beyond him. He decided to tell his most loyal, and devoted, counsellor exactly what had happened that afternoon, while the wan-faced Irishman listened.

At the end of his sorry tale, Myrddin sighed, as if the

wind had been knocked out of him. 'Then you did kill him.'

'It was a dreadful accident which has broken my heart!' the Prince cried. 'All I intended was to protect Daire. The only person at the lake with murder in mind was Gareth ap Iwan!'

'And I accept every word you say, my lord. But the first version of any story is the one usually believed and, here's the rub, Dafydd is adamant that Gareth attacked your friend because he was acting towards you in an unnatural way.'

'You mean he kissed me,' the Prince snorted.

'Gareth wanted to protect you from harm. That is what is being claimed.'

'What harm is there in it?'

The druid bit his lip as if making up his mind. 'Two men kissing?' he queried doubtfully. Then he added, 'It is true the Hebrew King David had his Jonathan, and the great King Alexander of Greece had his Hephaestion, but simple folk do not know this, nor do they necessarily think it excuses such behaviour.

'Humans are fickle creatures, my lord. Princes can be greeted with shouts of adoration one day, and jeers of derision the next.

'Overnight, smiles can turn to spittle. Demands are already being made for Daire's head to be brought on a platter to Gareth's widow. Some courtiers believe he has bewitched you.'

'And he has!' the Prince cried. 'I am mad with love! With his beauty and good nature, he has entranced me, and I have no wish for his hold over me to be broken. Ever!'

'If that is how you feel, your lives are in great danger. While he remains in Dyfed, Daire's existence hangs by a spider's thread. Try to protect him, and even you will be in peril, my lord. The choice before you is simple: your friend must return to his wandering exile or, if you wish to spend your lives together, you must both leave Arbeth and never return. Relinquish your position and, as you have no heir, appoint the Princess Rhiannon in your place. This is my advice, though I give it with a heavy heart.'

Rhydian's voice became tremulous as he said, 'And I thank you for it. Your counsel is always owl-like in its wisdom. What do you say, Daire?'

The Irishman's blue eyes overflowed as he replied, 'My love for you is tearing me to pieces! When I am in your presence, I can hardly breathe. I cannot eat nor sleep. I feel I was made for you alone, Rhydian. Though I have no wish to stay where I am hated, the thought of life without you is unbearable!'

'There is no question of that,' the Prince assured him. 'Once we have said our sad farewells to my sister, we shall slip into the arms of black night.'

'But where will you go? No welcome awaits you in Wales. That much is certain.'

'We will seek refuge at the court of King Anguish of Achren. Queen Elen is a good friend, and will give us sanctuary.'

The wrinkles on Myrddin's face deepened into furrows. 'There are princes in Wales, but I have never heard of a King Anguish.'

'How can that be?' asked the Prince. 'His kingdom is just three days' ride from here.'

'Achren is one of several names for the Otherworld, my lord. It is possible that you visited its rulers without being aware of the fact.'

The Prince was mystified. 'Can you explain this?'

'Even for me, it is a hazy and difficult subject,' the druid admitted. 'Celts know there is more to this life than what can be seen, heard and measured. We believe we are descended from the gods of the Otherworld and, at the end of our earthly lives, we will return to that land of youth and happiness. On very rare occasions, mortals can travel to Achren and return unharmed, and not be a day older than when they left. Members of that strange world-beyond-death sometimes venture into ours, and have dealings with humans. This is what must have happened to you, my lord, but how did you come to be acquainted with these monarchs from the Otherworld?'

'King Anguish persuaded me to exchange outward appearances with him so that he could rule Dyfed while I acted as his champion in mortal combat. For months, I took his place as High King of Achren and, now I come to think of it, most of the courtiers were young, tall and very good-looking. They feasted well, dressed in the finest clothes and jewels, and lived in great splendour.

'Existence was no paradise for the peasants. Anguish admitted that his rule was far from ideal, and confessed to learning much from his time here. You must have been, in part, responsible, Myrddin.'

'Undoubtedly,' the druid agreed, a thin smile lightening his grave face, 'but it is hard to credit that someone as shrewd as I did not realise we had a stranger sitting on the throne!'

'Was there a time, a couple of years ago, when I did not seem myself?'

Myrddin remembered the Prince's sickness and replied, 'Yes, you were tetchy and out-of-sorts for a while. The courtiers thought you were ill, and in pain. And I was convinced I had cured you of it with my herbal potions! Are you telling me that person was actually Anguish, King of the Otherworld?'

'It was,' Rhydian confirmed. 'I think it might be folly to tarry much longer, old friend. Do you have any magic sacks or spells to help us on our way?'

The druid's face turned as pale as quicklime. He shook his head and admitted, 'My lord, you are embarking upon a journey which is beyond the limits of my powers. Your father, Prince Maelon, was a great ruler because he relied upon his head and heart, not merely the whims of magic. You already do likewise without realising it.

He regarded himself as the servant of his people, rather than their master. By treating your subjects so well, you have done his memory proud. In future, ask the Force for Good for help. If there is any justice, it will look kindly upon you.'

The Prince dropped his eyes and murmured, 'Sometimes, I think I can hear my father's voice calling from the Otherworld. It makes me feel sad, and a little lonely.' Then he added more positively, 'But I shall take your advice. Now I have Daire in my life, we must learn to support each other, and use our talents to face whatever lies ahead.

'My sister's well-being will be safe in your hands, I know.'

A tear-drop plopped from the druid's aquiline nose. 'While I draw breath, I will do my best for her, my... friend.'

*

Whispers had reached Rhiannon long before the princes arrived in her bedchamber, so little explanation of their decision to go into exile together was needed. 'You could only kill someone in self-defence or in protecting another person,' she said. 'Good men do not commit murder. But I must confess, brother, that I had no inkling you also loved Daire.'

'My emotions were confused. Perhaps I was unwilling

to admit them to myself. This very day, I urged him to marry you! Our lives would have been simpler if he had agreed, but I doubt if any of us would have been truly happy.'

'To relinquish your throne for Daire is a sign of how deeply you must care for him. I need no persuading on that score, though I wish with all my heart that he wanted to be with me.'

She crossed the room and embraced the shy Irishman. 'You are the loveliest, most beautiful man I have met in my life, and I wanted to be your bride. If you prefer my brother, I cannot fault your choice. Like you, he is special. I wish great happiness to you both.'

With that, she kissed Daire on the lips for the first and last time. She hugged Rhydian and asked, 'When time passes and passions cool, will you come back to us?'

The Prince's face drained of colour so that it looked like a deathmask. The stubble on his chin stiffened as he admitted, 'The truth is, sister, we may never meet again in this world. Now, we must bid you the saddest of farewells.'

'Oh, do not say such a thing,' she moaned, as the princes left her.

*

Rhiannon felt as if she had fallen into a deep, deep pit of blackness from which escape was impossible. Sleep refused to release her from wretchedness. She lay restlessly, and recalled the moment she had first laid eyes upon the exquisite Irishman. For her, it had been love at first sight. His loss obliterated all her hopes of happiness. She began to weep, and could not stop.

The day's heat seemed reluctant to depart, and the night became oppressive and sultry. Flashes of lightning lit the sky, pursued by peals of thunder, but no relieving rain.

13

The Shimmering

The bowed and bloodied pair crossed Arbeth's bridge for a final time. After sleeping in each other's arms in the woods, they rode towards the place where the Prince had put the stag out of its misery, and begun his fateful journey to Achren with the High King.

'If we head from there to the north-east for a few days, we should reach Annwn,' Rhydian reasoned. 'We will take our time to allow your wound the chance to heal.'

Day after day, the royal pair meandered through Wales. With no sighting of their destination, and Daire's injury showing few signs of improvement, they became increasingly anxious. When they asked people for directions, nobody had heard of Achren. Rhydian silently begged the Force for Good to come to their aid.

The next afternoon, they came upon a lake much wider than any of those he had encountered on his journey with King Anguish. 'This cannot be the way. We only crossed one river and a few streams. I think it is time to turn back…'

A loud fart interrupted him. Its source was an old

man sitting on a bench outside a tumbledown hovel. Rhydian smiled at Daire and said, 'Very well, I shall ask that windbag if he can help us.'

As he approached the hairless-headed peasant, a pungent whiff assaulted his nostrils. The ancient one had not washed in weeks and reeked, but he immediately pointed at some distant hills on the far side of the lake when he was questioned by the Prince. He grinned, revealing a ragged row of rotten teeth and replied, 'Those are the mountains of Achren, but no-one ventures near them.'

'Why not?'

'Are you simple?' he sneered. 'That is where the dead folk go!'

'In spite of what you say, my friend and I wish to travel there, but we have no boat. Do you know where we might obtain one?' Rhydian enquired.

A gleeful look appeared on the man's face and he spat a globe of spittle onto the floor. 'Well, sirs, I possess an old coracle which I used for fishing when I was younger. You could have that. For a fee.'

'I will give you a silver coin.'

'I would not sell it for a gold one.'

'Then what is your price?' Daire asked suspiciously.

'You have fine horses, but they are of no use to you with a lake to cross. Let me have them, and I will gladly give you my boat.'

'Two of the best steeds in Wales in exchange for a crackle-skinned coracle!'

'That is my offer,' chortled the old man, and he belched, as if in celebration of it.

'I do not think we have much choice in the matter,' Rhydian intervened. 'If Anguish and Elen take us in, they will provide us with mounts and saddles. Very well, wrinkled robber, you have a bargain. Show us the boat, and we shall be on our way. There are still several hours of daylight left, and the lake is as smooth as a pebble.'

The coracle, like its owner, had seen better days. The leather-covering was cracked and worn, and there was only one oar. It was so small that the princes could just sit alongside each other on its central plank which formed the seating. The sun was shining warmly as they pushed off, and Rhydian began to paddle them from shore. Before long, Daire had to shape his hands like a cup to scoop out some water which had begun to seep into the bottom of the boat.

Things went well for a while but, when the sun cast its last rays and slipped beyond the horizon, they had only reached the middle of the lake. Daire's wounded arm was beginning to throb and ache caused by his increasingly frantic efforts to keep the craft afloat. Then the cold came down and began to bite.

Rhydian rested his chin on the end of the oar. He peered into the deepening gloom for the nearest place to land and rest, but bands of cloud were obscuring the rising moon. A drawn and anxious look covered his face. All he could see was a pinprick of light so far away that it seemed pointless to shout for assistance but, when it drew nearer and nearer, the princes began to wave and cry out, 'Help us!'

The shimmering closed upon the coracle. Gradually, they could make out a figure, shining with spectral fire, walking on the water. At last, Rhydian realised they were witnessing a spirit on its way from Achren. 'It is a ghost,' he whispered. He began to sweat and shiver at the same time. 'And it bears Gareth's face! I fear we are about to meet the fate which I inflicted upon him!'

The princes exchanged a desperate look. The oncoming apparition made their blood run as cold as midwinter. Even when it came within touching distance of the boat, the phantom remained silent. Then, to the petrified friends' astonishment, it offered each of them an earthenware bowl which had been tucked beneath its arms.

The companions accepted the vessels, and the spectre finally spoke. 'Use these to bail out the lake water. Stay afloat until sunrise, and all will be well.'

'But I thought you were the spirit of Gareth ap Iwan whom I drowned,' Rhydian ventured.

'I am.'

'Why then are you being so kind? I thought you had come to watch us perish.'

'As you did me?'

'And I bitterly regret what I did to you that day. Defending Daire did not require me to be so violent. How sorry and ashamed I feel is beyond my words.'

'I have been a member of the Otherworld for a short time, but I already realise it was a mistake to react so angrily to your kiss, the most genuine expression of earthly passion. Love, whether it is between a man and a woman, a man and a man, or a woman and a woman, is what really counts and is a blessing. It was wrong of me to see an act of tenderness as a curse and a source of dishonour. What good would revenge do me now? I have forgiven you, though there was not much to forgive.'

A radiant moon lit up the sky, and seemed to smile upon the relieved Prince who readily agreed with the ghost's sentiments.

'That is my feeling on the matter too.'

'It is never easy to cross from your world into ours, but I am sure we shall meet again in Achren,' said the spectre before it turned and moved away.

The grateful friends did not speak nor rest until they had made the boat safe. Then they hugged each other for comfort and warmth.

*

At dawn, a brisk breeze began to blow upon their backs. The rheumatic coracle danced across the lake and beached itself on shingle. The princes jumped ashore, stretched their stiff legs, and then scrambled up a steep slope of granite rocks to the top of the closest hill. In the distance, and glowing in the morning sunshine, Rhydian recognised the copper-coated spires of the palace of Annwn.

'At last!' he shouted.

14

The Otherworld

The dishevelled travellers encountered an unexpectedly hostile reception when they reached the ramparts of the capital.

'Who are you, and what do you want?' called a burly guard.

'We are the princes of Dyfed and Ulster, and wish to meet the High King and Queen. They are good friends.'

The sentry roared with mocking laughter. 'And I am the Emperor of Rome! You look like scarecrows! Where are your horses, and crowns, and jewels? Be off, you dishevelled loons, before I let the dogs out! You have no place here.'

'Please send a message to Queen Elen telling her that Rhydian, Prince of Dyfed, awaits without. It would go well with you, if you were to follow my wishes.'

There was something in the young man's tone that wore authority, and the sentry had second thoughts. 'Very well, but you will remain outside until I have received Her Majesty's orders.'

Eventually, the wooden gates of the capital groaned open, and the strangers were escorted into the great hall which Rhydian recalled with some fondness. Anguish recognised him immediately, as did Elen, although she thought the Princess Rhiannon's sketch of his likeness did not flatter him in the least. If anything, he was more attractive than she had imagined.

The High King's greeting was lukewarm, almost cold. 'Why are you here? Nobody, not even a prince, is allowed entry to Achren without expressed royal permission.'

'The truth is, Sire, we have been sent into exile from both our countries, and have received no hospitality elsewhere. We hoped,' and the Prince looked imploringly at the Queen, 'that you might take us in as guests.'

His beseeching glances touched Elen's heart. She would have loved him to stay, but knew it was impossible. She tried to explain. 'In many ways, as you will recall, life here is like your own, Rhydian, but there are countless courts in the Otherworld, some much finer than this…'

'And a few are little better than that of Dyfed,' interrupted the High King. 'You are not yet destined for the afterlife and, when that time comes, you will be spending eternity elsewhere.'

'But my husband can grant you a dispensation to stay for a time,' the Queen said, and she gave Anguish an admonishing look. 'From what you have told us, it would be a kindness to allow you to recover from your recent ordeals. And we do our best to be generous to those in need.'

Gratitude lit Rhydian's face, and he thanked her sincerely. Then he turned to Anguish and said, 'Sire, I do not understand why you were so reluctant to fight Leare. Surely, the High King of the Otherworld cannot be killed.'

'Oh, it can happen! Not often, it is true, but there are times when a member of our country ceases-to-be. We cannot take eternity for granted. The Underworld also exists. The lives of the lowest peasants in Achren are much sweeter than those doomed to the hell that is Hades. Only the gods, in their palaces above the mountain-tops, are truly immortal...'

In an attempt to lighten the serious mood, the Queen said, 'My lord, let me order a special banquet, with honeyed wine, in honour of our royal guests. I will see to the preparation of their bedchambers personally.'

Daire spoke at last. 'We need just one, my lady.'

The Queen's fair eyelashes flickered and her smiling lips thinned, but her only comment was, 'Then I shall ensure it is our finest.'

*

During the days which followed, much of the princes' time was spent in the field chasing deer and the sharp-tusked boar. They enjoyed the companionable rivalry of the chase, though they did not adore it as gleefully as the High King who seemed to live for its thrills. 'That was a good kill!' he would bellow at the top of his voice.

Anguish's hounds came to like Rhydian enough to

lick his hand. They allowed him to pat them and, when he groomed their shining fur coats, their ears glowed redder than the reddest rose.

Daire grew stronger, and a new layer of skin formed over his wound. Thanks to Myrddin's ointments, there was only a scar to show on his arm where there could easily have been a stump. In the evenings, he serenaded the Queen with Irish songs and poetry.

She returned the compliment by playing melodies on the harp, and singing in a serene voice which enchanted everyone.

Time drifted by, and the princes began to forget their troubles and disappointments. Life in the court of Achren suited them very well.

One morning, however, the High King announced, 'Sadly, my friends, it is time for you to return to your own world. I have given you as long with us as I dare. The gods are growing impatient, and I have no wish to anger them.

'Go to the lakeside where a boat awaits you. It is watertight and has a sail, so your journey homeward will be much safer than the one on your way here.

'My wife has a headache, and is a little tearful today. She has asked me to bid you farewell on her behalf. I have enjoyed your company, but she has delighted in it, and will miss you very much. Though sad to see you go, we both wish you good health, and great happiness, in your life together.'

*

The skiff skimmed across the lake at such a speed that it was not long before the princes were tying it fast to a rotting, wooden jetty a short distance from the old man's dilapidated shanty. When they saw their horses still tethered to a nearby tree, they grinned at each other. Daire's white mare's mane shone in the sunlight. She remained docile as they approached, but Rhydian's powerful stallion reared, kicked and snorted with excitement.

The hovel's door creaked open and the ancient peasant emerged, looking red-faced and feverish. He sneezed several times, shooting snot into the sky, before shouting, 'Who is disturbing my horses?' Then he recognised the princes and continued, 'Those wretched beasts were a waste of my time! Nobody can get near them. When I showed your stubborn mules to hopeful buyers, that lunatic grey maimed one with his great hooves, and bit a chunk out of another!'

The Prince realised it was impolite to laugh, but could not stop himself. 'It serves you right, old thief. But we have need of our mounts, so will exchange that skiff beside the lake which, unlike your coracle, is sound and sturdy, for our horses. It is small, manageable and has a sail so, even at your advanced age, you might consider fishing again.'

The peasant's face brightened. His skin crackled like

parchment when he grinned. A little drool dribbled down his chin as he chuckled, 'You have a deal, sirs. And I have a bargain!'

15

Prince of Nowhere

Exile. A year of rejection passed while the royal couple rode through the valleys, and round the coast, of Wales. The warmth and joy of the Otherworld stood in stark contrast to reality. Wherever they went, they were treated like poison. Such dreadful lies had been spread abroad by the evil-minded that no-one made them welcome. They were forced to head further and further into the mountains of the north.

One morning, Rhydian peered through a milky haze to the island of Ynys Môn and muttered, 'If we venture there, we will be shunned like vipers.'

Daire kicked some damp soil over the embers of their overnight fire. 'Why?' he asked.

'That is where Myrddin's magic bag turned the villain, Llwyd ap Gwyn, into a fox to enable me to rescue my sister. His eyes were fixed upon Rhiannon so he did not pay me, disguised as an old peasant, much attention but, if he were to recognise my face, I fancy it would become a target for his fist!'

'Where else is there for us to journey? Only one jewel remains in your scabbard for us to sell, but we are young and fit, and do not fear manual labour. As long as we can be together, I should be happy to be a swineherd.'

Rhydian laughed. He put his arm around Daire's slender waist, and kissed his lips tenderly. 'Maybe we are no longer called princes, but I never wish to see, or smell, you in a pigsty! Very well, my friend, desperate times call for desperate measures. Let us venture to the land of druids and see how we fare. It would be difficult for our luck to become worse.'

*

To cross the Menai Straits, the princes waited at a ford for low tide. The eddying and rushing of the current disturbed their steeds, and they had to be driven into the water. When they all reached the safety of the far shore, the stallion whinnied, stamped his hooves and shook his sodden coat vigorously, showering Rhydian from head to toe.

Before they arrived at Llwyd ap Gwyn's fortress, the princes hid their horses and swords in a nearby wood so they bore no resemblance to royalty. They approached the gate, and were met without suspicion. A guard nodded them through, saying, 'My lord is in need of servants. If you are willing to work, the master himself will receive you.'

To their surprise, they were escorted into the great hall where the fiery-haired lord, who now sported a beard of similar hue, sat on a wooden throne. Rhydian thought he exuded a more sober air than he had in their last meeting. When the chieftain glanced up at him, he frowned and then guffawed. 'For a moment, I thought you were that rascal, the Prince of Dyfed!' The hall resounded with laughter when he added, 'You will not turn me into a badger, I trust!'

Rhydian blushed, but feigned innocence. 'No, my lord. I am Huw, and this is my Irish companion, Conor. His Welsh is limited so, if I may, I will answer for us both.'

'Do you realise that I require vassals who are not afraid of labouring?'

'We will serve you in any way, my lord, if we could but live here in your household.'

'Certainly not!' Llwyd asserted, irritated by such a forward suggestion. 'The servants' quarters are small and reserved for my most trusted men. You will have to find your own lodgings outside the fortress. Widows are often in need of a tenant or two.

'Your young friend can start in the scullery. Perhaps he will furnish us with an Irish dish or two. You look and speak well, Huw, so you may serve at my table. Start at dawn, tomorrow.'

The princes looked into each other's shining eyes and smiled. They followed the chieftain's instructions to the letter. Daire sweated in the sweltering heat of the kitchens, but found that he enjoyed cooking, and made some suggestions about Irish recipes which received a welcome at high table. Meanwhile, Rhydian knew exactly how to wait upon a member of the nobility, and his charm soon made him a favourite.

They tried living with a widow who needed assistance with her goats, but they disliked the lack of privacy. With a little gold from the sale of their last ruby, they found themselves a remote smallholding where they kept bees for honey and chickens for eggs, and lived in a damp roundhouse of the kind in which peasants dwelt.

*

For several months, they enjoyed their good fortune. At last, the gods seemed to be favouring them.

Then Llwyd's mother, Lady Olwen, returned from an extended visit to her married daughter in Harlech. As soon as she strode into the great hall and laid eyes upon him, Rhydian sensed that she knew his identity. Fearing the worst, he was relieved when she swept past without a word.

One glance of the Prince's emerald eyes had been enough. The Lady Olwen summoned him directly to her chamber for a private interrogation. The tangle of tension in his gut made him feel nauseous.

'I am astonished that, in my absence, Llwyd has given you, of all people, a position at court,' she declared. 'Why has the Prince of Dyfed come here posing as a servant? Clearly, there is mischief afoot!'

Rhydian's face flushed a foxglove pink. An unconvincing liar, he saw little point in trying to outwit this shrewd woman. 'The truth is, my lady, that the Prince of Nowhere stands before you. I have been driven into exile, and am now your son's most devoted and loyal liegeman.'

Lady Olwen snorted, 'Why should I believe a word you say? You deceived us once before by coming here and pretending to be a peasant. Perhaps you should have thought of something more original this time. You almost broke my heart when you turned my son into a wild animal.'

'Because he acted like one in his treatment of my sister!' Rhydian retorted. 'He dragged Rhiannon here against her will, having threatened to kill many innocent women and children. What else could I have done? My duty, as a loving brother, demanded nothing less.'

His outburst silenced Olwen because it rang the bell of truth. When the heat at her forehead cooled, she reluctantly admitted, 'There is much in what you say. I warned Llwyd against invading Dyfed for the sake of a woman who had rejected him. It was wrong.

'So was trying to force your sister into marriage. But he adored her, and still does! The Princess is a special woman. She has the gifts of beauty, wisdom, sweet speech and more. Truly, I wish she did return his love.'

The lady cupped her hands over her cheeks as though

trying to contain the exasperation which her wayward son caused. 'Llwyd lacks the gift of patience. He should have waited before asking for her hand again but, I can assure you, he is a much finer man now than the arrogant, impulsive youth you first met.

'Twenty-four hours in total, terrifying darkness has cured many of his faults. Believing he was entombed alive, and would never see his loved ones again, has caused him to see the world in a very different light. Most of his vanity and arrogance has gone, his childish obsession with military matters has ebbed to a mature interest, and he no longer renders himself senseless with too much mead and wine.'

Rhydian had heard enough. 'I agree with you! My lord would make a much finer impression upon my sister. I remember her finding his appearance agreeable enough.

'The only welcome we have received in the length and breadth of Wales has been on Ynys Môn. Even as servants, we have been treated justly. If you will permit it, my friend and I would be more than content to continue living and working here. All we ask is that we remain known as Huw and Conor.'

His pleading eyes were difficult to resist. Like the distant rumbles of thunder after a storm has passed, Olwen's anger faded.

When the frown left her face, the Prince's hopes rose. 'Very well, I will allow you to stay for the time being.'

She hesitated and then asked, 'The Princess is married by now, I assume?'

'Not as far as I know, my lady, though it is quite some time since I laid eyes upon, or heard news of, her. Would you like to send a message to Dyfed informing Rhiannon of my whereabouts and suggesting, now your son's nature has improved so much, that she pay us another visit?

'I have a rudimentary skill in writing, and can add a few lines in my own hand, emphasising how kind you and your son have been to us. This would weigh heavily in his favour. I will assure her that she will be treated with due respect. To see her again would be wonderful.'

His mistress's grave face was transformed by a smile like a sunbeam, and she cried, 'Yes, it would! It is uncommon for a nobleman to be able to read and write. How is it that you do so?'

'As you know only too well, my lady, noblemen are taught to be warriors, not scholars. Most of my boyhood was spent learning to ride, and to wield a sword, shield and spear, but my mother was determined that I should also be able to read. She persuaded Myrddin, our wisest druid, to commit a little of his knowledge to parchment, and then to teach me the basic skills of literacy. Some people believe I devoted too much time to the arts of poetry and music, at the expense of the science of warfare.'

'How will your sister know that the message is not a ruse to entrap her?'

'I shall recall some intimate incidents from childhood.' His voice wavered when he went on, 'If I include a few details about our parents' deaths – they suffered shaking fits and loss of the use of their limbs, probably caused by hemlock poisoning – she will be convinced of its truth. Have you a messenger upon whom you can depend?'

'My manservant, Gwilym, is trustworthy,' she answered.

Rhydian slipped a gold amulet from his sturdy bicep and offered it to her. 'Tell him to hand this to the Princess herself. It is a charm to ward off evil which she gave me in happier times. The triple spirals of good fortune have been wonderfully worked on it. She will recognise it straight away. If I know my sister, she will be as anxious to meet Daire and me again, as we are her.'

The Lady Olwen took the golden band and exclaimed, 'There is no time to lose!'

16

Horn of Truth

When Gwilym gave Lady Olwen's letter, complete with Rhydian's postscript and charm, to the Princess, she was bewildered, but delighted. Shocked to learn of their humble stations, her brother and Daire were safe. That was what really mattered. Better to be poor and happy than rich and unhappy, she reasoned.

To see the princes again, she was prepared to journey to Ynys Môn. Being the guest of that vain and arrogant fool, Llwyd ap Gwyn, whose violent nature she despised, was a price worth paying. She trusted Rhydian. He could not be tortured into penning that it was safe for her to visit, if it was not. His crabbed handwriting was unmistakable, as were the personal memories he had included.

*

Several weeks later, the Princess's carriage, which had four wheels, an arched wooden roof and some leather suspension straps to cushion the ride, lumbered along the rough tracks of mid Wales. It was accompanied by a small retinue of guards and servants. Progress was snail-like so she had ample time to think about the possibility of the northern chieftain being a reformed character. She found it very difficult to believe.

Bugles blew and jugglers tossed and caught flaming brands when the royal carriage finally turned into the courtyard of Llwyd's fortress. Servants and courtiers cheered, and Rhiannon was made to feel like an empress from some exotic country. As she stepped down, she pulled back her hood and revealed her lovely features, drawing shouts and whistles from the onlookers. She gave a nervous wave, and the noisy throng yelled its approval even louder.

Long, swarthy hair dangled in two braids over her slim figure which was cloaked in ruby-red. The open-mouthed host was, once again, overwhelmed by her beauty. He bowed deeply and said, 'We are delighted by your arrival, my lady. How my mother has persuaded you to visit us, after the appalling manner in which I treated you on the last occasion, is beyond me. What I did then was unforgiveable, even though I did it from a misguided expectation of your hand in marriage. Now, I realise you cannot compel love. It has to be freely given. But, believe me, when I say I am older and wiser, and will ensure your stay will be a memorable one.'

The Princess was pleased by the change in the nobleman's tone and manner. He was tall and well-built, and she had a fondness for men with sorrel hair, but she spent most of his welcoming words looking unsuccessfully for Rhydian. She had to wait until the banquet that evening to see him.

Once Llwyd had escorted Rhiannon to her seat beside him and the feasting began, a voice came over her shoulder which she recognised immediately. 'Would you care for some rainbow trout, my lady?'

Rhiannon laughed quietly but, before she could reply, the chieftain intervened, 'You are to be attended by Huw as he is my best servant.'

'That is most thoughtful of you, my lord.' She turned to Rhydian and said, 'Yes, I would, Huw. It is a particular favourite of mine,' and the royal siblings exchanged knowing winks.

The feast was a merry affair. When Llwyd rose to make the formal toast to his guest, he was greeted with some raucous encouragement from his courtiers. In front of the Princess lay a jewelled drinking horn from which she, and her host, were to drink. Into its mouth, and seen only by her brother, she slipped some shining crystals.

The chieftain picked up the vessel and filled it with wine. He held it aloft and began a very different speech from the one he had made on the Princess's former visit. Swagger and arrogance had been replaced by a humility and gentleness which Rhiannon found almost unbelievable.

'Mother and welcome guests,' he cried, 'I ask you all to stand and drink to the health and happiness of our distinguished guest, Rhiannon, Princess and ruler of Dyfed!'

The packed hall rose as one and the shout went up,

'Rhiannon, Princess and ruler of Dyfed!' Great gulps of wine or ale were swallowed, including one by the lord himself, to celebrate her presence. Llwyd then passed the horn to his guest who raised it, and drank the remainder of its contents. By so doing, she convinced her relieved brother that the crystals could contain nothing evil.

'We are here tonight to make amends for the shameful way in which we – or more accurately, I – treated her on a previous occasion. Now, I deeply regret acting without regard for her feelings. When you love someone who does not feel the same way about you, it is hard to accept, but it does not excuse the cruel and reckless behaviour of which I was guilty.

'In the presence of so many witnesses, I beg the Princess to forgive me.' He turned to Rhiannon and vowed, 'On my honour as a nobleman, I swear never to treat you in such a despicable fashion again. I further promise not to lead an army into battle unless it is to protect the innocent. Fine words are much easier to say than fine deeds are to do but, henceforth, I will try to follow the golden rule: behave toward others as you would have them do to you.'

Prolonged cheering rang out until he took a small gift from his tunic and handed it to the Princess. It was a silver brooch with a magnificent emerald embedded into it. 'Please take this as a token of my admiration and respect.'

Rhiannon stood and received the present graciously.

Gratified by his thoughtfulness, she said, 'I forgive you,' and kissed him lightly on the cheek.

*

Before the end of a tiring day and the welcome embrace of sleep, the Princess sent her maid in search of the servant who had attended her at the feast. When he arrived in her bedchamber, they hugged so long and closely that it almost became difficult to breathe.

'Sister, it is wonderful to see you again. I believed I might never do so. When you accepted the contents of Lady Olwen's letter and agreed to journey here, Daire and I felt blessed by the gods.'

He paused and asked, 'What did you slip into Llwyd's drinking-horn? I feared it might be poison!'

Rhiannon laughed. 'Nothing so dramatic, brother. They were crystals of truth. Myrddin insisted I bring them with me to Ynys Môn. When mixed with liquid, they have the magical property of making anyone who drinks them tell nothing but the truth. I was anxious to know Llwyd's real thoughts and feelings. It seems you are right. Incarceration in utter darkness has transformed his character. Thanks to the crystals, I can be certain of it.'

'Are there any left?' Rhydian asked. 'They might prove useful, in future.'

'None remain, I am afraid. Myrddin said they are

scarce and precious, but gave me all he had. They have served their purpose.

'Henceforth, I shall look upon Llwyd more favourably.'

A mischievous twinkle appeared in Rhydian's eyes. 'Would you consider accepting his hand in marriage?'

Rhiannon shook her head, but the thought of it made her heart skip a few beats. 'It is far too early to say such a thing!' Then she added, 'His features are well-proportioned and his physique is most manly. Now that he has discovered how to smile, he has his attractions, I have to admit.

'It is time to hear of your adventures, brother. Tell me everything.'

*

The Princess lit a flame in the chieftain that burnt as brightly as a candle. They often went riding together. They danced, and Llwyd proved athletic and accomplished at it. He was always attentive, apologetic for his past misdeeds and generous with compliments. Members of his household noticed that a permanent smile seemed fixed to his face when he was in her company, and her eyes shone whenever she looked at him. Upon greeting, they not only bowed and curtsied, but began to embrace each other.

Days turned into weeks. Rhiannon postponed her

departure on two occasions. Rhydian had never seen his sister look happier or more beautiful. She laughed so much in her host's presence that it was obvious she was beginning to share his feelings.

17

Morgen

One dreary morning, when a bank of leaden clouds threatened rain, Llwyd persuaded Rhiannon to take a ride with him. Before they had ventured far, drizzle began drifting in the wind. Later, the sky assumed a slate-grey scowl and the droplets deepened into a downpour. The couple dashed for shelter under the canopy of a copper beech tree.

Accompanied by the patter of raindrops, they chatted amiably, until they were interrupted by a woman who appeared before them as if from thin air. Somehow, her elegant clothes were bone-dry. She was wearing a white mantle, with a silky smock next to her olive-sheened skin. A circlet of gold, in the shape of a snake, decorated her long, black hair, and silver sandals adorned her feet. Her looks bore a striking similarity to those of the Princess, except her eyes which were a grey so pale that they were almost colourless. On her right cheek was a beauty spot which acted like a magnet upon most men.

'Welcome, my noble lord, Llwyd,' she said, in the sweetest voice imaginable. She looked at him, ignoring Rhiannon. 'Please do me the honour of visiting my humble home to escape this inclement weather. It is a short distance from here, in the woods.'

Fascinated by this strangely attractive lady, the chieftain asked, 'How do you know my name? I feel sure we have never met before. Pray tell me yours.'

'I am Morgen, my lord, and understand all that is worth knowing about you. With one glance, I have seen your innermost secrets and wishes. Until you set eyes upon me, you thought you loved the Princess of Dyfed, but I have turned your feelings upside down. The only woman you now want stands before you clad in white and silver and gold. Confess it!' she demanded.

Llwyd scoffed at her brazen claim. 'I will only admit to loving the Princess Rhiannon above all others.'

The siren rejoined, 'Prove that you do not find me irresistible.

'Come to my home for a meal. The invitation extends to your mute companion.'

The nobleman responded with a harsh laugh that sounded like a bark. 'I am not as fickle as you suppose.' He turned to Rhiannon and asked, 'On such a miserable day, would some food be welcome, my lady?'

The Princess stared into Llwyd's hazel eyes and decided to see how this man, who professed his love for her so loudly, reacted to the attentions of such a temptress. 'Yes, my lord, as it is some hours since we broke our fast.'

They entered what seemed a modest building with a thatched roof, but, once they passed through its door, they looked upon a palace whose walls were decorated with tapestries featuring the naked figures of Celtic gods and goddesses. Brilliantly-coloured banners hung from a high ceiling which glinted with gold. The floor-space was furnished with a huge table groaning with sumptuous food and wine, a huge bath filled with crystal clear water from which whisps of steam rose, and a huge bed covered with a shining quilt. Rubies, emeralds and topazes were strewn across the marble floor like confetti.

Morgen invited her guests to sit at the table. Llwyd marvelled at the banquet laid out before them and said, 'If the fare tastes as well as it looks and smells, it will be delicious.'

A succession of pretty maidens brought them wonderful delicacies to whet their appetites. Then dish after dish appeared; roast meats, game pies, eels and crabs, pasties and exotic fruits. The wine-jugs seemed to be bottomless. Even the Princess had never been entertained so royally. The food and wine began to make her feel drowsy, and she drifted into a profound sleep. The chieftain shook her, but without effect.

'Desist! A sleeping-draught has ensured she will not wake till tomorrow. By then, you will be mine. Come, my sweet lord, bathe and sleep with me. From now on, your life will be one of endless pleasure. What is more, we shall remain young forever.' After the hostess made these alluring promises, she slipped the mantle from her shoulders, and stood before him in the sheerest smock, revealing her shapely figure.

'No!' he protested. 'I want to grow old with my beloved Rhiannon!'

His retort enraged Morgen who glared at him menacingly and warned, 'Do as I say or neither of you will escape from this place save what the ravens bear away in their claws!'

Before she could thunder any more, Llwyd swept the sleeping Princess into his arms and bounded across what seemed an endless floor towards the grand portal. The threat, 'Come back! No mortal can deny me!' chased after him.

The ground suddenly began to quiver and shake as in an earthquake. Chunks of rafter and ceiling crashed to the ground, one glancing his back on its way. Get out! Get out! was all he could think. An unearthly wailing noise rent the air, and stabbed his eardrums like a sharp needle. The screeching sound seemed to take all substance out of the structure. As it collapsed in an eruption of dust, the chieftain managed to stumble across the threshold into the welcome arms of the rain.

Still holding the Princess in his protective grasp, he surveyed the heap of rubble, mud and thatch but there were no signs of life or bodies. The ruins were eerily empty.

The shock of the dank air failed to revive Rhiannon. When the effects of the sleeping-potion wore off, she found herself propped upright, and locked in the chieftain's embrace. They rode slowly back to his fortress, a rope tied to her trailing horse. He told her of Morgen's plan to steal him away, and his reaction to it. 'Trust me, Princess, she never tempted me to abandon you. Not for a second.'

And, even without the truth crystals, Rhiannon did believe him.

She gazed wide-eyed at the reassuring face of her rescuer and said, 'I fancy the gods sent a wraith to test your faithfulness, and you have passed with colours flying, my love.'

*

Eventually, the Princess's duties obliged her to tell Llwyd that she could delay her return no longer.

At once, he knelt upon one knee and pleaded, 'Do not go back to Dyfed without me, my lady! All I desire is to be your husband. Take my hand in marriage, and I shall become your vassal. I will follow your orders like the lowliest subject, if you will agree to be my wife.'

The Princess was moved by his request, and made up her mind in an instant. She was ready to embark upon the voyage of love and marriage and, without hesitation, followed her heart's prompting.

A radiant smile lit her face as she exclaimed, 'Yes, Llwyd, I accept your offer! You will become the next Prince of Dyfed, nothing less. We will rule together as equals.

'Your mother will miss you, so we shall have to make regular expeditions to your estates.' She realised that this would also enable her to visit her beloved brother, and Daire.

The Lady Olwen squealed rapturously, like a little girl, when told the news of her son's betrothal. 'A wedding! You have made me the happiest of mothers!' she cried, and she hugged the breath out of him. Hot and flushed, she could feel her heart beating so fast she had to calm herself. She vowed, 'I will ensure you are the finest-attired bridegroom in the whole of Wales! Of course, your bride will need no help on that score.'

*

For several days, the great hall glittered with the best gowns, and the finest gold rings and brooches in Gwynedd. Wine, mead and ale flowed freely, and servants carried heavily-laden dishes from the fiery kitchens. Only when the stocks of food and drink ran dry did the colourful and clamorous celebrations of the forthcoming marriage come to a close.

Then the happy couple set out for the south-west. Olwen joined Rhiannon in her two-seated carriage so they could discuss the wedding plans in detail. She was already making preparations for the arrival of her first grandchild. The Princess laughed at her enthusiasm, but secretly shared it.

The future Prince of Dyfed, looking splendid in scarlet and gold and assured in the saddle of a black stallion, rode ahead. A retinue of horsemen and running servants accompanied him. Their task was to scout and ensure that the way was safe. They kept a close and wary watch on their lord, his lady and mother. All made an impressive sight.

As the train of carriages and carts trundled into the distance, the former Prince of Dyfed sighed sadly. Content that his sister seemed destined for happiness, he wiped a tear from his eye.

18

Captives

'This is Mona, the island of druids, savage priests who conduct human sacrifices every day! Give no quarter to these barbarians!' a centurion barked at his legionaries. 'Roman discipline and courage have already driven these creatures inland. Our task is to fell the oak-tree groves where their abominable rituals take place.'

Accompanied by swooping seagulls and swimming horses, his men had paddled their specially prepared, flat-bottomed craft across the shallows of the Menai Straits. Even the most experienced soldiers, who came from all corners of the Empire, were feeling apprehensive. A row of long-beaked cormorants, with their black wings outstretched to dry, did not seem a good omen.

The weather was humid. In helmet and armour, and carrying a spear, shield and stabbing-sword, they were sweating like pigs. The Celtic tribesmen were poorly armed and trained, but they were formidable, if foolhardy, warriors. Romans could take no risks with them.

*

Early next morning, the centurion sent out Gaius, his most experienced decanus, with a small detachment of men to scout and, if opportunity arose, forage for food.

After a short march, the legionaries chanced upon a roundhouse surrounded by hives humming with bees, clucking chickens and several tethered goats. They smiled greedily. Though panting a little from his exertions, the decanus himself landed a couple of kicks on the wooden door, which quivered and shook before falling open. Expecting to find a Celtic family at home, the veteran was astonished to discover two young men in a bed, and lovingly entwined.

'What is going on?' he yelled.

The startled princes jumped up and gaped at the intruder who was wearing a magnificent helmet adorned with red, white and black feathers, and an impressively armoured uniform. He was speaking a language neither of them recognised. Naked and unarmed, they were unsure how to react. Eventually, Rhydian said, as calmly as he could, 'I am Huw, and this is Conor. You are welcome in our home.'

Gaius could not understand a word of Welsh, but he was familiar with its sounds. What was striking about these men was how handsome they were. They had faces and lithe torsos to rival those of the statues he had seen in Rome. He wondered if they might be Celtic gods.

More legionaries entered the hut and stared at the odd couple. A slim Nubian, who possessed a skin much darker than any the princes had ever seen, suggested that they be allowed to dress before being taken prisoner. But a short, thickset soldier, whose face had turned a shade of purple, raged, 'Honour and duty above all things! That is the Roman way. Such men behave worse than beasts.

'They dishonour their nation. Let us do the druids a service and kill them!'

'I give the orders here, Marcus,' Gaius declared. He was not convinced that the men before him were mortal. 'They look like gods to me. The dark-haired one is the very image of Apollo. I dare not order their execution.'

'Gods, my arse!' bellowed Marcus. 'They are cowering like rabbits! I will prove they are men – just like us.' With that, he leapt across the hut and landed a punch on Rhydian's face which split his upper lip. Crimson coursed down his chin.

'What did I tell you?' the triumphant legionary shouted. When his cry was greeted with a gale of laughter, his nostrils flared wide with pride and pleasure.

The muscles on Gaius's face did not move. He refused to be beaten and commanded, 'Take them prisoner! They might have useful information for our officer. Tie their hands, but do not clothe them. A little humiliation is in order.'

*

The Roman soldiers dragged their captives, and some slaughtered animals, back to the camp which was already surrounded by a ditch and wooden palisade. The decanus led them to the centurion, a gaunt, middle-aged man with greying hair who was wearing a red cloak, breastplate, leather kilt and greaves on his legs. 'Who are these men and why are they naked?' he demanded.

'They are Celts, sir. We found them in bed like this, kissing like a married couple.'

The officer's eyebrows arched. 'Really? Have they told you anything about the local chieftain?'

'We do not understand a word they say, sir,' Gaius replied.

'Summon a translator, at once,' his superior ordered. His bony face looked serious. 'I will get something out of them before they die.'

When he recommenced, he stared at Rhydian's bloodied face and asked, 'Who are you, and what is your status?'

'I am Huw, and this is my Irish friend, Conor. His Welsh is poor so it would be best if you were to interrogate me,' he suggested, in the hope that he might protect Daire from harm. 'We have a hut, raise a few animals and live off the land. Our existence is humble, almost hermit-like.'

'In other words, you have been shunned by your own people because of your contemptible, deviant ways. Tell me about your chieftain.'

'I know he is named Llwyd ap Gwyn. That is all.'

'You are a lying scoundrel!' the officer roared, a dangerous red inflaming his face. 'You must have been to his hill fort at sometime. How many men does he command?'

'I have no idea.'

Question upon question rained down upon the Prince for over an hour, but he told his inquisitor nothing of military consequence. Eventually, the centurion wearied and admitted, 'This is a waste of my breath. I cannot discover what is going on in his pretty head, but I doubt if he knows much of importance. They can take any secrets with them to Hades where their flesh will be torn from their bones by hundred-headed beasts. Execute.'

'What form of execution, sir?'

'Well, they are hardly royalty,' the centurion sneered. His eyes rolled malignly as he added, 'Outcasts, little better than slaves. Let us make use of them to show the natives of this forsaken island to expect no mercy from the glory that is Rome.

'Tomorrow morning, take them to the nearest hill so their punishment can be seen for miles around. Two bodies left hanging to rot, like a farmer's rats, should serve as an effective warning. Crucify!

'Now bring me a cup of wine. I need something to banish my cares.'

19

A Roman Solution

Daylight began to fail. Countless stars sprinkled the sky and a crescent moon shone. The night grew colder. A damp chilliness engulfed their naked bodies, and the captives started to shiver. Then the Nubian legionary appeared. He provided them with water, chunks of barley-bread, and blankets, enough to keep them from death's grasp.

After giving him thanks, Daire peered at his dark, smooth skin and added, 'I have never seen anyone who looks like you. From where do you come?'

A broad smile lit the African's face when he held out his upturned hands and shrugged his shoulders, as if to say, 'I do not understand.'

*

Following a few hours of fitful sleep, it was a cheerless waking at dawn. The ropes binding the prisoners' wrists were untied so they could each carry a beam of wood, perhaps twelve feet long. A slave, who seemed used to the role of porter, balanced two shorter, slimmer planks on his shoulder. The princes had no idea what purpose this timber served, but they were relieved to be released from their bonds, and freed from the gruelling interrogation.

Gaius told the Nubian to bring along a bag full of tools and some six-inch spikes.

The awkward length and weight of the wood soon began to take its toll on Daire who was less sturdy than his companion. He toiled and sweated up the hill but, when his pace began to slacken, Marcus yelled, 'Move faster, you Celtic bitch!' and lashed his back and legs with a leather whip. Every swipe of the soldier's arm made the captive wince and left an angry red weal.

'Hold your hand!' Rhydian cried. 'He is not an animal! There is no need for such barbarity! I can help carry his load as well as my own!'

The Romans neither comprehended nor appreciated his protests. Marcus moved his attentions from Daire, only to begin thrashing the Prince instead.

By the time they reached the summit, their bodies were dripping beads of sweat and blood. Daire noticed a glint of the Irish Sea in the distance and wondered what his father, the King of Ulster, would say, if he could see him now.

The prisoners were given a few moments to recover their breath. Then they were handed short-handled spades and instructed to dig two deep slit-trenches. While they hacked at the stony ground, the legionaries used the iron spikes to nail the timbers together to form two T shapes. The princes were still unaware of the purpose of the items of crude carpentry which were lying flat on the ground.

The decanus waited for the holes to be finished. When he nodded at Daire, the soldiers grabbed the innocent, pushed him down onto the wooden structure and forced his arms to stretch out against the crossbeam. They bound his wrists to it, and his ankles to the larger upright, until he was tied securely into place. Several men began to heave the T into the air until Gaius shouted, 'Wait! Take no pity on him. Nail his feet to the cross. This is the centurion's order. He said the prisoners die too quickly without support.'

Marcus grinned and, as instructed, started to hammer home several spikes. When the excruciating pain struck, and blood began to run, Daire's dreadful shrieks and screams echoed across the island. As the upright was raised, the hill seemed to spin, and his head rang like a bell. The base of the cross was dropped into one of the trenches which was infilled with earth. A couple of supporting stakes ensured its stability.

While Daire dangled in midair agony, Rhydian lay motionless on the ground. The moment the legionaries had begun to tie his lover to the tree, he had flown at them like an eagle trying to protect its young. He managed to land several powerful punches before a blow by Gaius, from behind his back, had turned day into night.

A fuzzy light returned, and Rhydian thought he might

never move again. The chills of the earth had crept into his body which was aching intolerably. As his senses cleared and his vision began to focus, he realised that he was being bound to the second cross.

An almighty crash accompanied a spike smashing through his ankle, followed by a searing agony so intense that the trauma of it almost caused him to blackout again. He remained vaguely aware of being hoisted upwards until he was almost within touching distance of his friend.

Daire was sobbing, moaning and murmuring prayers to the gods. A mixture of tears, gore, sweat and urine was dribbling from his body into a muddy puddle beneath him. The gentle Irishman was broken. For a while, he had used the strength in his arms to keep at bay the rising tide of liquid in his lungs, but his muscles were failing. As he began to drown, drawing a breath became torture.

Soon his spirit would depart, so he gasped, 'I had hoped to be with you for many years, Rhydian... The gods have not seen fit to allow it... but every moment with you has been so precious that I bless my father for sending me into exile...'

He uttered nothing more.

Tears trickled down the Prince's cheeks. 'Do not fear the death we are about to face, my love. Shortly, I will follow you into the Otherworld, and we shall spend eternity together,' he vowed.

When the angelic-natured prince gave up the ghost, a brilliant light shone briefly around his head. Then a mist, like a floating grey veil, descended and clung to the crosses. The hilltop was suddenly, and violently, icy.

Summer became winter. So dramatic was the transformation that the unsettled soldiers began to mutter in a mutinous manner. Marcus moaned, 'At this rate, we are going to be here all flaming night.' He reinforced his point by spitting in the decanus's direction.

'My patience is exhausted,' Gaius growled, his dark eyes glowering angrily. 'No man here wants to leave this godsforsaken spot more than I do, but you know perfectly well, that we cannot return to camp until they are both dead. Only then can we leave them to feed the birds.'

'In that case,' Marcus cried, 'I will have to hasten his end!' He snatched a spear in his powerful hand and thrust it into the prisoner's midriff. When he angled the tip upwards and pushed hard, it pierced Rhydian's heart.

A bolt of lightning streaked across the sky. The Romans left this place of pain and punishment to a tattoo of hailstones. In the distance, a vixen howled. Then a raven landed on the Prince's shoulder, and began to gouge out his green eyes.

20

Rhiannon's Lament

I have been where Rhydian was slain,
Son of Maelon, extolled in song:
When ravens screamed over blood.

I have been where Daire was slain,
There is no hiding my sadness:
When ravens screamed over flesh.

I have been where Celts were slain,
Ribs broken and shields shattered:
When ravens screamed over battle.

I have been to the door of Death,
Where blood-soaked ravens screamed:
I am alive, they in their graves.

William Vaughan

BLOOD MONTH

£4.95

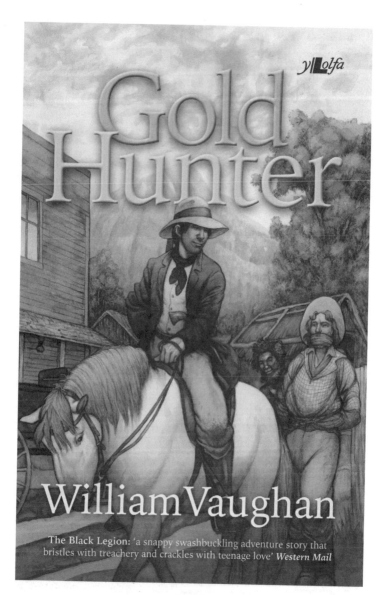

y Lolfa

Gold Hunter

William Vaughan

The Black Legion: 'a snappy swashbuckling adventure story that
bristles with treachery and crackles with teenage love' *Western Mail*

£4.95

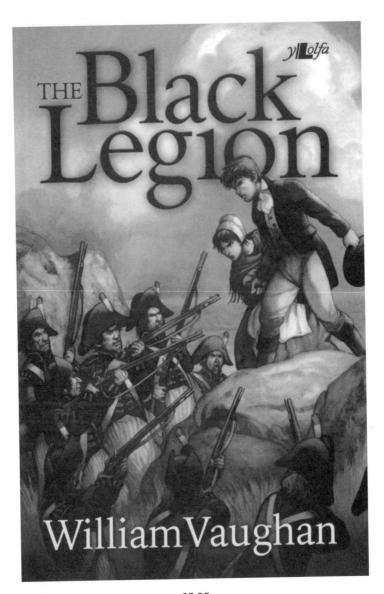

THE Black Legion

William Vaughan

£5.95

When Ravens Screamed Over Blood is just one of a whole range of publications from Y Lolfa. For a full list of books currently in print, send now for your free copy of our new full-colour catalogue. Or simply surf into our website

www.ylolfa.com

for secure on-line ordering.

TALYBONT CEREDIGION CYMRU SY24 5HE
e-mail ylolfa@ylolfa.com
website www.ylolfa.com
phone (01970) 832 304
fax 832 782

Printed by Y Lolfa
Ask for a quote